THE
HITCHHIKING
VAMPIRE

THE HITCHHIKING VAMPIRE

Stephen Mooser

Delacorte Press

Published by
Delacorte Press
Bantam Doubleday Dell Publishing Group, Inc.
666 Fifth Avenue
New York, New York 10103

Library of Congress Cataloging in Publication Data

Mooser, Stephen.
    The Hitchhiking Vampire / by Stephen Mooser.
        p.   cm.
        Summary : En route to join their mother in the desert, thirteen-
    year-old Jamie and her older brother pick up a hitchhiker with a
    bag of money and soon find themselves helping to place a $12,000
    bet in Las Vegas.
        ISBN 0-385-29725-4
        [1. Las Vegas (Nev.)—Fiction. 2. Gambling—Fiction.] I. Title.
    PZ7.M78817Hi   1989
    [Fic]—dc19   88-29406
                                                                  CIP

Manufactured in the United States of America

May 1989

10 9 8 7 6 5 4 3 2 1

BG

For my friends who made the drive:
Jim Dobbs, John Ezmirlian, Alan Heimel,
Tom Massey, Norman Zimmerman

CONTENTS

1

IT WAS SURE SOME PARTY

Not far from San Diego a wooden castle called the Hotel del Coronado sits at the end of a long white beach. It's one of the fanciest places I've ever seen. And surely one of the most famous. It's always in the news for one thing or another. Maybe you saw pictures of it during last year's National Music Awards, held in its big dining room. And back in February I saw it on an episode of *Spy for Hire*. I know it's been in the movies too.

I also know this: The people who run the hotel won't ever forget my thirteenth birthday party. And neither will I.

It all began early on the evening of June twenty-fourth with my father escorting me and my sixteen-year-old brother, Luke, through the hotel's tall oak doors. If you remember the dining room from the Music Awards show, then you may recall the high domed ceiling and huge crystal chandeliers. What you may not have seen was all the polished wood and brass, the bouquets of red roses, and the fine paintings that hang on its walls. It was the most elegant place I'd ever seen. And the most intimidating.

Of course, it didn't intimidate my dad. Nothing ever did. When he came through those doors on that fateful June day, his head was high, and his voice so clear and assured you would have thought he owned the place.

"It's my daughter Jamie's thirteenth birthday," I remember him announcing to the thin, sharp-nosed maître d'. "Get me the best table in the house, my good man, and at once!"

I must confess his confident attitude had me worried. That's because both Luke and I knew that dear Dad didn't have a cent to his name. Fortunately, because we were dressed to the teeth, our lack of cash was not immediately evident. Dad was a real dandy in a black tuxedo and ruffled white shirt, Luke was wearing his best gray suit, and I even had on a dress, a new fluffy one plastered with roses and daisies. Dad had made me buy it earlier that day, and every time I looked down at it now I felt my face flush. When you're used to jeans and a T-shirt, you can't help but feel uncomfortable dressed up like a flower farm.

Maybe Dad wasn't cowed by that fancy hotel, but Luke and I sure were. And for good reason too. Only four years earlier we'd all been living in a shack outside of Peabottom, Missouri. None of us had ever seen the inside of a McDonald's, let alone a place like the Hotel del Coronado. Then someone discovered lead under our land and suddenly we were rich, or at least it seemed that way. We'd picked up and moved to San Diego and Dad had taken on the airs of a lead baron. The money, what there had been of it, was just about gone now, but Dad hardly seemed to notice. He just kept on spending, and when the bills came due he neither paid them, nor paid them the slightest mind.

The maître d' gave us a sugary smile and waved to a bald, stumpy waiter, who scurried over, picked up three menus, and showed us into the gigantic room.

"Would the gentleman prefer a window seat?" he asked.

"Certainly not," said my father, turning up his nose as if he were the grand duke of San Diego. "That large table over there, in the center of the room, is where we'll sit. I want my daughter not only to see, but also to be seen."

"But, sir," said the waiter, "that table is for a party of ten—or more."

"We'll take it," said my father. He pulled out a chair and nodded for me to be seated. "We'll eat for

3

ten, I assure you. Bring us a round of cold lobster and caviar appetizers, sparkling waters for my two guests, and for myself—a gin martini, straight up.''

I looked over at Luke and rolled my eyes. Big trouble was in the works. When Dad got to drinking, anything could happen and usually did. If we got out of the Coronado with our skins that night, I'd count it a miracle.

"Order anything you want, sweet pea," said Dad. He reached over and patted me on the hand. "And don't you worry about the cost. This is your birthday."

It was hard not to worry. After all, we didn't have the money to even pay for the soda water. But since I knew it was pointless to argue, I went ahead, ordered, and hoped for the best.

The food turned out to be first rate. Luke and I stuffed ourselves, and enjoyed the good times while they lasted. Between courses, and martinis, Dad made friends with some of the people at the neighboring tables, passing out advice on San Diego's best restaurants and entertaining them with tales about the history of the Coronado. The stories sounded reasonable enough, but they just as easily could have been made up. Dad was never shy about twisting the truth, especially if it made for a better story.

He was in the middle of a tale about the San Diego Zoo when he suddenly rose to his feet, placed his hand on the shoulder of the blue-haired woman he'd been talking to, and announced, ''Be back in a minute, sweetheart. Got to go to the bathroom.''

''Oh, well, uh, please ...'' stammered the surprised woman, but before she could complete her reply Dad had staggered away.

Luke tugged nervously on his ear, then leaned across the big table. ''Jamie,'' he whispered, ''let's ditch him before he comes back. Otherwise it's going to be just like the Ritz.''

The very thought of the Ritz sent a shudder through my body. That was another meal we didn't have the money for. We'd gotten out of paying our huge bill there only through use of what Luke and I later referred to as the ''Ritz Trick.''

''Sweet pea,'' Dad once told me, ''people will do most anything for a dollar. Make fools of themselves, lie, cheat. Anything. Remember it. Someday it'll save your neck.''

It had sure saved Dad's neck that day.

The bill had been for something like two hundred and forty dollars, but all Dad had was forty of it, and all in singles. Just as the bill arrived that evening I remember he stood up and loudly announced that he was from Texas and he'd just discovered an ocean of oil under his property.

''Hee haw!'' I remember him shouting. ''Everything is on me tonight!'' And with those words he began whirling through the Ritz tossing dollar bills into the air, laughing wildly as the money fluttered about like leaves on the wind.

You wouldn't have believed the way those rich people started scrambling about for those dollars, waiters too. Right at the last I even remember the door to the kitchen opening up and a half a dozen cooks and dishwashers come tumbling out for the free loot.

As for us we just waltzed right on out of the restaurant and slipped away into the night. Amid the confusion no one had noticed us go. The Ritz Trick, it had worked all right a few months ago, but it wasn't anything I ever cared to repeat. Especially not on my birthday.

"Anyway," Luke was quick to point out, "at the Ritz, Dad had forty bucks in his pocket. I don't think he's got more than a dollar or two on him tonight."

I shuddered again but said, "We can't leave. It would break his heart. He means this to be my birthday gift."

"Some present. We're all going to end up washing dishes to pay for it. With my luck I'll probably cut my hand on a broken glass and end up in the hospital. Before I can get out of there, no doubt I'll pick up some horrible disease like leprosy, and then, just as I—"

"Luke! For heaven's sakes, you're not going to get leprosy just because Dad's short of cash," I said, shaking my head.

My brother had to be the world's greatest worrier.

Anytime there was a problem, he had a way of imagining the worst possible thing that could happen.

He crumpled up his napkin and dropped it on the silk tablecloth.

"I just wish Mom hadn't had to go to Utah this summer to take care of Grandpa. She'd know how to get us out of this mess."

"How? With a joke?" I said.

I was serious. Mom's way of dealing with a bad situation was to make people laugh, hoping they'd forget what they were fighting over or worried about. It didn't always work, of course, but many times it did. I remember one time when we were still living in Missouri she and Dad had gotten into a terrific fight about money.

They were nose to nose, shouting at each other about a three-dollar mop, when Mom suddenly cried, "Next time maybe I should buy the mop the same way smart people buy canaries."

"Canaries?" Dad said, scratching his head. "How do smart people buy canaries?"

"When they're going cheep!" chuckled Mom.

By the time Dad stopped laughing, the fight had been forgotten. She and Dad were now divorced, but she still used the trick trying to break up arguments between me and Luke, or sometimes, as she liked to say, "just to chase the blues away."

"Don't worry, Luke, soon as Grandpa gets better Mom will come home," I said. "Anyway, maybe Dad found some money in the washroom."

Luke smiled. "Jamie, look at him," he said, nodding toward my father as he weaved our way. "Does that look like Mr. Moneybags to you?"

As a matter of fact it did. Even when he was broke, Daddy always managed to look like a million bucks. His clothes were from the finest shops, his hair was always cut by the best barber in town, and he even had his nails done by a woman down at the Ambassador Hotel. Drunk as he was, he looked good even now, save for one minor flaw. His fly was open.

"Dad," I whispered, soon as he sat down. "You forgot to zip up your pants."

He gave me a big wink and reached under the table.

"Thanks, sweet pea." He smiled.

While we'd been eating, the big room had filled with people, and I could see a bunch of others waiting by the door to be seated.

"Dad." I smiled. "I want to thank you for the birthday, but I think we'd better get going. Looks like they could use the table."

"Let 'em wait," said Dad coldly. "We're not done with the party yet."

I tried to keep up my smile, but felt the corners of my mouth starting to turn down. Dad could get ugly when he'd been drinking, especially if he thought someone was trying to tell him what to do. To even suggest a change in his plans would usually push him off in the opposite direction. In fact, before their divorce, Mom had usually gotten her way only by suggesting they do just the reverse of what she wanted.

But then, suddenly, Dad brightened, leaned back in his chair, and poked a finger toward the high, vaulted ceiling. "First thing, sweet pea, we got to have a little cake. And second thing, we got to sing a little 'Happy Birthday.' What do you say?"

I leaned across the enormous table and shook my head. "Dad, please," I whispered. "Can't we finish the party back at the apartment?"

"Jamie's right," said Luke. "Back at the—"

"Shut up, Luke," said Dad. "This is your sister's party."

Luke pulled on his ear and wilted into his chair. For a moment everything was real quiet. It wouldn't have surprised me a bit if he had suddenly ripped into my brother. Dad loved to make a scene. Loved to be the center of attention.

Anyway, I was expecting the worst when Dad suddenly caught sight of a pastry cart coming our way.

"Ho!" said Dad, signaling the puffy-faced Pillsbury Doughboy look-alike pushing the cart. "Bring that thing over here."

"Sir?" said the waiter, wheeling the cart up to my dad. He picked up a pair of silver tongs and waved them over the tray of fancy cakes. "What would the gentleman—"

"Ah-ha!" said Dad, reaching out with his bare hands and plucking off a gooey jellied pastry. "This

9

looks perfect." The shocked waiter dropped his tongs and watched, open mouthed, as Dad plopped the pastry onto the tablecloth, licked off his hand, and launched into a loud, off-key stab at "Happy Birthday to You."

"Dad, please," I said, but the old souse pretended not to hear. Turning to the blue-haired woman at the next table he said, "It's my daughter's birthday. it would really thrill her if you'd sing along."

The woman set down her fork and smiled sweetly, "What's your daughter's name?" she asked.

"Jamie! Jamie Plufphanger," said Dad in reply. Then, cupping his hands to his mouth, he shouted to the Coronado's surprised patrons. "Attention, diners! Now hear this! Extra! Extra! It's Jamie's thirteenth birthday. Let's everybody sing!"

Waving his hands about as if conducting a symphony orchestra, Dad began singing in his loudest voice. A few people at nearby tables joined in halfheartedly, but most people stared into their food, pretending not to hear.

"I said sing!" shouted Dad. "Come on, folks. This is for my daughter."

Pounding the table in time with the music Dad raised his voice in song once again. Past experience had taught me that the time had arrived to clear out, but no sooner had I begun to slide my chair away from the table than Dad called me back.

"Young lady! Just where do you think you're going?"

Before I could reply, the maître d' was at Dad's side, our bill in hand.

"I'm sorry, sir," he said, "I must ask you to leave. I'm afraid you're creating a disturbance."

"A disturbance!" he snarled. "I'm paying a small fortune to eat your overpriced swill. I'll darn well do what I want."

"Please, sir. If you'll just leave quietly. I—"

Dad glared up at the maître d'. "I'd appreciate it, fathead, if you'd leave." He lowered his voice to a whisper. "Quietly."

The maître d' stiffened. "Sir, if you don't leave now I'll be forced to call security."

"Security!" roared Dad. Thrusting a hand into the air he leapt to his feet. "You have me arrested and I'll sue this dump for every last thing in it—including the grease on its cheap spoons."

Now every single eye in the place was focused on my father, and for a moment everything stood still. Then, Dad took a step backward and a very surprising thing happened.

For, as it turned out, Dad had accidentally zipped the tablecloth into his pants when he'd come back from the bathroom. So, when he stepped back he pulled the tablecloth halfway off the table, upsetting the glasses, sending most of the dishes crashing to the floor, and splattering the maître d's pants with jellied pastry.

I gasped with disbelief as I stared at my father,

planted as he was in the middle of the Hotel del Coronado with a tablecloth flowing out of his trousers.

The maître d', his face as red as the jelly sliding slowly down his pants, looked primed to explode. But somehow he pulled himself together and once again presented my father with the bill.

"There will be an additional charge for the china," he said. "You may pay at the door."

"I prefer to pay right now," said my father calmly. And without further warning he stepped forward and punched the surprised gentleman in the face, sending him to the floor amid the ruins of my birthday feast.

Dad wheeled about and flipped Luke the car keys. "Go get the car," he barked. "I'll meet you out front."

What next followed I'm not too sure, for the entire dining room suddenly erupted in chaos. Chairs fell over, glasses broke, screams and curses filled the air. Not far away I saw a pair of security guards come charging out of the kitchen. But before they'd gotten ten feet they'd collided head on with a swarm of panicked diners heading for the exits. The pastry cart went over with a clatter, the fire alarm went off, and someone with the voice of an opera singer began to scream. And in the midst of all this was my father, struggling toward the front door with the tablecloth streaming behind him like a bride's silken train.

Hitching up my dress I grabbed Luke by the arm and scooted out the nearest door and into the parking lot. The car was where we'd left it and we jumped in and drove around to the front. Poor Dad, however, never joined us for the getaway. When next he appeared he was in the custody of the San Diego police. I watched sadly as they threw him into the back of a black-and-white police car and then sped away into the evening, siren screaming, lights flashing.

"Thanks for dinner," I mumbled, waving half-heartedly at the disappearing squad car. "It was sure some party."

And so began my fourteenth year. I'd like to say that as far as excitement goes it was all downhill after that night. But that simply wasn't the case. In fact, I was about to be launched on the most amazing adventure of my life.

2

ON THE ROAD

The next morning I got a call from Dad at the apartment we shared with Mom.

"Hello, sweet pea," he said. "Bad news. The clowns down here at the courthouse are going to lock me up for thirty days."

"Thirty days?" I said.

"Can you believe it?" he said. "I barely tapped that maître d'. How was I to know the guy couldn't take a punch?"

I shook my head. "Do you want us to come down?"

"No, please don't," he said. "Might be bad for my fatherly image. Know what I mean?"

"I'm sorry this had to happen," I said.

"Don't be sorry for me, sweet pea," he said. "Save your tears for the del Coronado. When I'm done suing them I'll own their hotel. Heck, this was the best thing that could have happened to me. Our fortune's made."

I said I'd keep in touch and then hung up. Poor Dad, though maybe it was all for the best. At least in jail he'd have a chance to sober up. Let's be honest here. The man was a maniac when he was drinking.

After lunch I reluctantly called Mom in Utah. I never liked to phone her with bad news, because she was an even worse worrier than Luke, and I knew my call was sure to upset her.

It did.

"Your father started a riot at the del Coronado! Heavens! Did anyone get hurt?"

"Only the maître d'. Dad slugged him pretty good," I said.

"I was an idiot to leave you in that madman's care," said Mom. I imagined her running a hand through the halo of curls surrounding her plump face. "That settles it. I'm getting you both out of there today. Jamie, put your father on the phone."

I explained that he couldn't come to the phone for a month.

"You mean you're there alone? Jamie, this is terrible."

"Mom, I'm telling you we're fine. Please, don't worry."

"Don't worry! How can a mother not worry when her babies are left abandoned on the streets? Oh! Your father!"

"Can you come back?" I asked. "Is Grandpa better?"

"Grandpa's still pretty depressed," she said. "I really can't come. You and Luke are going to have to come out here, on the bus."

I groaned. "The bus!"

"What's so bad about the bus?" she said.

"Everything," I said. "Why can't we take the car? Luke can drive, and we can pay for the gas with Dad's credit card."

"It's too far. I'd be worried sick."

"Mom, you know what a safe driver Luke is."

"Luke isn't the one I'm worried about."

"Mom ... please ..."

"We'll see." She sighed. "Put Luke on the phone."

Luke got on and said, "Yeah, I guess so.... Sure, Mom.... Don't worry, Mom.... Yes, I'll drive carefully." Pausing, he looked over at me and winked. "Yes, yes, I'll keep her out of trouble, I promise.... We'll call along the way. Okay.... The woman who was dying? No.... Yeah, very funny, Mom. I'll tell her.... Okay, see you soon."

He hung up the phone and gave me a kind of half smile. "Looks like we're driving to St. George, Utah. Sound okay?"

"Are you kidding!" I said. "It sounds great. When can we leave?"

"In the morning," said Luke. "By the way, Mom wants to know if you heard about the woman who thought she was dying?"

I rolled my eyes. It was time for Mom's joke of the day. "No," I said. "What happened to her?"

"She went and sat in the living room and felt a lot better," said Luke.

I groaned, as I often did at Mom's jokes, then said, "That does it! Next Christmas I'm buying her a jokebook."

We packed the next morning. I put a dress in the suitcase, but for the trip I wore my summer uniform: patchwork jeans, a San Diego Padres T-shirt, and pink and blue socks—a pink one on the right foot, a blue on the left. I brushed my teeth, ran a comb through my hair and grabbed the newspaper off the dining-room table. I was ready to go.

When I got outside I discovered Luke's long, gangly body bent under the hood of Mom's Pontiac. I rested my elbows on the fender and peered in. "Anything wrong?"

Luke's sad blue eyes gazed out at me from the gloom. "Just checking the radiator. We don't want to break down in the desert. This car isn't exactly new, you know."

I patted the fender. "She'll make it."

"She'd better. Otherwise we're going to find ourselves fried up like bacon on the sands of the Mojave. Or worse yet we could try to hike for help and fall into a forest of cactus. Can you imagine ten thousand cactus needles stuck in your—"

"All right, Luke," I said. "I get the picture, okay. Don't worry. This car's in great shape."

Luke snorted and slammed down the hood. "I wish I had your confidence."

Five minutes later we were heading down Mission Boulevard, with Luke behind the wheel and me behind the *San Diego Union*. Ever since I can remember I've started the day with the paper. I don't understand why everybody doesn't. Really, the stuff they put in there just about beats any made-up story you'd read in a book or see on TV. I read the whole thing, of course, but during baseball season I always start with the sports. For the last two years I'd been following the San Diego Padres, the local baseball team, and I never missed a story about them in the *Union*. I heard their games on the radio when I could, and I'd even been out to Jack Murphy Stadium to see six of them in person. They'd been cruising along in first place for most of the season, but they'd recently lost four out of five games and had slipped to second, behind the Los Angeles Dodgers.

I slapped my hand against the paper. "Can you believe it, Cardoza is still playing Anderson at third. When is that manager ever going to learn that that turkey can't field? How dumb can you get!"

"A lot dumber," said Luke. "He could be trying to

get to St. George, Utah, on seventeen dollars and a credit card. That, now, would really be the height of stupidity—don't you think?''

"Seventeen dollars?'' I said. "Is that what we got?''

"That and Dad's credit card.''

"Doesn't sound so bad to me,'' I said.

"Sure, if nothing happens,'' said Luke. "But what if—''

"Luke, stop worrying,'' I said. I sighed and put down the paper. "You know if Dad was here he wouldn't be thinking about the money. He'd be too busy having a good time. Let tomorrow take care of itself, isn't that what he used to say?''

"Used to,'' said Luke. "Before that great philosophy of his got him thirty days in the slammer.''

"You laugh, but it doesn't hurt to take a few risks,'' I said. "Remember how Dad used to always say, 'Nobody ever won a drawing who didn't take a chance on a ticket.' And what about Lightfoot Hobbs? Do you think he would have ever made it to the Hall of Fame if he hadn't taken chances and stolen all those bases? Of course not.''

Luke shut his eyes for a moment and shook his head. "Tell me, Jamie, do you ever think about anything besides baseball?''

"What else is there?'' I said, smiling.

Mom had driven us to St. George the previous year, so the route was fairly familiar. Nevertheless, I kept referring to the California map I found in the glove compartment and used it to navigate us out of San Diego and onto Highway 15. Once free of the city the highway took us along through the low, rolling hills that bordered the Anza Borrego Desert. I put down the window and let the warm air swirl through the car as we passed through a string of towns with names more fit for Mexico than the U.S., places like Tierrasanta, Rancho Bernardo, and Mira Mesa.

By and by the country gave way again to pavement and shopping malls, the road widened out to six lanes, and we found ourselves smack in the middle of Riverside, a town that may have once been pretty, but was so thickly smothered this day by smog that it was impossible to see more than a few blocks. After Riverside it was on through hot, sprawling San Bernardino and then countryside again as we started to climb through El Cajón Pass, ten thousand feet high and gateway to the giant Mojave Desert.

The pass was much higher than I remembered and the mountain it crossed never seemed to end. Every time we'd round a corner, another mile or so of steep grade would come into view. Up we went and so did the temperature gauge. As the needle climbed into the red, little whiffs of steam began puffing out from under the hood.

Hunching over the wheel Luke tried to talk the car over the hill. "Come on, baby," he said. "Almost there now. You can make it. You can make it...."

I felt like a passenger on the Little Engine That Could.

Up the hill we chugged, with the car spitting steam like a cracked boiler. By the time we spotted a Shell station near the top of the grade, the car had slowed to a crawl. Somehow Luke coaxed the car off the freeway and we rolled into the station looking like a hot white cloud on wheels.

The gas-station attendant, a turkey-necked kid with a huge Adam's apple, came over and peered into the geyser of steam roaring out from under our hood.

"Looks to me like you've overheated," he said.

"Duh," said Luke, as we climbed out of the car.

"This pass is tough on old cars," said the attendant. He walked over, picked up a hose, and handed it to me. "Here, you can use this to cool it down."

While Luke filled the car with gas, I lifted up the hood and splashed some water on the radiator. Before long I'd raised up a cloud of steam that all but swallowed me up.

"Why, I bet you folks are the fifth car today to pull in here like this," came the attendant's words through the mist. "Hotter'n buttered grease in a skillet, ain't it?"

When the world came back into view again the attendant was still talking a streak. His Adam's apple bobbed up and down like a cork on a stormy sea. "You kids going to Vegas?"

"St. George, Utah," I said. "We're going through Vegas, though—if the car holds out."

The Pontiac took nine dollars and fifty-seven

cents' worth of gas and Luke gave the kid Dad's credit card.

"You'd better let that wreck cool down for a while," he said. "You can park it over there, if you want, by the phone booths."

Luke gave me fifteen bucks and I followed the attendant into the station and picked out lunch, some cheese, apples, and a carton of milk.

When I went up to the counter to pay, Mr. Adam's Apple gave me a strange, cold look and totaled up the charges.

"Twelve dollars and seventy-seven cents." he said.

"Twelve dollars for apples and milk?" I said. "Give me a break."

"Three twenty for the food, nine fifty-seven for the gas," he said. He passed me Dad's credit card. "This card's no good. Look, it's expired."

I gazed down at the card in horror. He was right. It had expired two days earlier. Wouldn't you know it, though. Even when Dad wasn't around he had a way of stirring up trouble.

"Twelve dollars and seventy-seven cents," he repeated.

I gave him a ten and a five and went out to the car to tell Luke the news.

"Oh, that's just great," he said. He tugged absent-mindedly at his ear. "I got maybe two bucks in my pocket. How we going to get to Utah on that?"

"There's a sign inside that says Vegas is less than

two hundred miles away. We can be there in four or five hours.''

''Then what?'' said Luke. ''Put the two dollars in a slot machine and hope for the best?''

I opened the door and climbed inside. ''Of course not,'' I said. ''We'll put the money in a pay phone and call Mom. She'll send us gas money for sure.''

''I don't know,'' said Luke.

''Come on, live a little,'' I said. I shook my head and gave him a look of disgust. ''If Dad was here, you know what he'd say?''

''Please, spare me his dumb philosophy,'' said Luke. He started the car. ''If we break down between here and Vegas, I just want you to remember one thing.''

''What?'' I said.

''That it's your funeral,'' he said.

Two hours later we met a crazy man.

3

THE HITCHHIKING VAMPIRE

At least he looked crazy. Heavens, it was 120 degrees in the desert and this old coot was just walking along the road, halfway between Barstow and Baker, in the middle of nowhere, and I mean nowhere, walking along the road.

According to the map we were just over the hill from Death Valley, which gives you an idea of the kind of country we were driving through. Outside of a few thirsty-looking bushes all you could see for miles and miles was sand and rock. If I didn't know any better I might have thought we were on the moon.

Anyway, we could see this guy from a long way off.

"Mercy," I said. "Can you believe someone's actually walking around out here?"

"I see it, but I don't believe it," said Luke.

"We ought to stop and see if he's okay," I said. "Slow down."

"If he wasn't okay he wouldn't be walking," said Luke. "Don't you think we've got enough troubles without picking up hitchhikers?"

"Pull over, Luke," I said. "Anyway, he's not hitchhiking, and I didn't say we had to give him a ride. Maybe he just needs some help."

The closer we got, the clearer he became. Long white hair stuck out from behind the blue cap he wore on his head, and he had on a pair of white coveralls that looked plastered with pockets. There was a big paper bag in his hand.

"Maybe he's collecting aluminum cans," Luke said. Despite himself, he began to slow the car.

"Pull over," I said. "He might need help. Please."

Luke looked at me as if I'd slipped my rocker, then squinted out at the old man. "Are you kidding? The guy could be a murderer. For all we know he's just come back from burying the last people who gave him a ride. Who knows, maybe he even—"

"Come on, Luke. He's just an old man. For all you know he could be dying of thirst. Pull over."

"Picking up hitchhikers is dumb, Jamie."

"Is it dumb to save someone's life?" I asked. "You

can't just pass him by. Stop. All I want to do is talk to him. Find out if he's all right.''

Luke gritted his teeth and pulled onto the shoulder. We coasted along slowly till we came alongside the old man. Then I leaned out the window.

''Need any help? Something to drink? A ride?''

The old man stopped and eyed me suspiciously. And I must admit I did the same, and for good reason, because—well, you might not believe this, but, I swear, on first inspection I thought the old guy was a vampire. I guess the thing that startled me most about him was his dark red lips. And, when he opened his mouth, I got another jolt. His teeth were cracked and all jaggedy, just like Dracula's. I would have told Luke to hightail then and there if the rest of his face hadn't been so pathetic looking. His skin was as brown and wrinkled as the paper bag in his hand and his eyes were so sad and tired looking you would have thought he hadn't slept in years. Everything about him, in fact, looked kind of old and beat up, everything, that is, but the cap on his head. It looked practically brand new. And I was surprised I hadn't noticed it earlier, for it advertised the Los Angeles Dodgers, the Padres' big rival.

''Hey, what do you know, a Dodgers fan,'' I said. ''What do you think about 'em trading Rusty Nelson to Houston?''

''You going to Baker?'' he asked in a gravelly voice.

''We're going to St. George,'' I said, ''but we'll be

going through Baker.'' I stared at his lips for a while, decided he wasn't Dracula after all, and asked, ''You okay?''

He sighed and licked at his dry red lips. ''I've done better,'' he said. He glanced up at the sun. ''Heat's pretty bad.''

I turned back to Luke. ''We ought to help him out, don't you think?''

''Jamie, I don't know,'' said Luke.

The old man looked a little dazed, as if the sun had been working him over for the last few hours.

''Well, we just can't leave him here,'' I whispered. ''It would be criminal to drive away now. He won't last another fifteen minutes in this sun. Just look at his eyes.''

Luke squinted out the window and studied the old man for a good minute or two.

''I guess you're right,'' he whispered. ''He does look a little shaky. We sure can't let him die.''

I smiled and leaned out the window. ''So what do you say, want a ride?''

The old man bent over and peered cautiously into the back of the car, as if he was expecting to find it full of snakes.

I unlocked the back door. ''Get in,'' I said. ''Come on. You must be dying of the heat.''

He finally climbed in, bringing with him the odor of sagebrush and dust, and made himself comfortable in the back.

He was just about the strangest old coot I'd ever seen. His overalls had so many pockets on them, you couldn't hardly see anything else. And those lips, those red lips, were just plain weird. He hadn't been in the car more than a minute or two when he stuck his hand in one of those pockets and came up with a handful of tiny red nuts that I recognized right off.

"Those pistachios?" I asked.

He held out his hand. "Come all the way from Iran," he said. "Want some?"

I plucked a pair of the nuts out of his wrinkled hand and put one in my mouth.

"Healthiest things in the world, pistachios," he said. "No nut in the world is as nutritious. They got every one of the essential amino acids. Every one, and that's a fact."

"You get 'em in Iran?" I asked.

He smiled and showed off his cracked teeth. "I get them in Baker. Manager of the market there special-orders them for me. Course, they grow them over the hill in Bakersfield now, but they're not as tasty. Less clams, though, I will say that."

"Clams?" I asked.

"Nuts with shells that haven't already been cracked," he said. "Splitting 'em open can be kind of hard on the teeth." He smiled and showed me what the clams had done to his choppers.

"Most pistachios I've seen are white," I said.

"Folks don't like the way the red ones stain the

lips," he said. "But that don't bother me none, not where I come from."

Luke looked at him in the rearview mirror.

"Where would that be?" he asked.

He gazed off into the desert. "A little place back in the mountains."

"What town?" I asked.

"No town," he replied. "Just me, plus a million or so lizards and snakes."

"You must be a Dodgers fan?" I said.

"Dodgers?" he said. He threw a handful of shells out the window.

"The L.A. Dodgers," I said. "You wearing one of their caps."

He took off the cap and looked at it as if seeing it for the first time. "Oh, this," he said. "I found it on the highway. Must have blown off someone's head."

"They're not doing too well this year," I said.

He gave me a quizzical look.

"The Dodgers," I said.

He licked his lips. "You folks got any water? I'm perishing of thirst."

"No water," I said, "but we got some milk." I handed him the carton. "Here, take all you want."

He drank it dry in three gulps. Then he realized he'd drained the carton and his eyes grew big. He said, "I'm—I'm sorry. Looks like I drank all the milk. There ain't none left."

"That's okay," I said, thinking it wasn't okay at all. That milk was going to be half our lunch.

"Here," he said, reaching into his paper bag and drawing out an old dollar bill. "I want to pay for this."

"That's okay," I said.

"No, no," he said. "I insist."

"Jamie," said Luke, "take the dollar."

He dangled the rumpled bill in front of my face till I finally plucked it from his hand. "Thanks," I said.

We rode along in silence for a few minutes, but curiosity about the old man finally got the better of me and I turned around in my seat, stuck out my hand, and said, "My name's Jamie Plufphanger and this is my brother Luke. We're on our way to Utah to see our mom. I don't think I got your name."

He smiled and said, "Call me Hank."

"You planning on staying in Baker?" asked Luke.

"I ain't planning on staying at all," he said. "Vegas is where I'm heading, but Baker is where I catch the bus."

"Vegas!" I said. "Why, we're going through there." I looked at Luke. "Maybe Hank can ride with us."

'I don't know," said Luke. "The extra weight might be more than this old car could take."

"I'm willing to pay," said Hank. "The bus will cost me ten dollars, and I'd just as soon give it you as Greyhound."

Luke swallowed and studied Hank in the rearview mirror. "We do need some money," he said.

"And if you're worried about the weight," said Hank, "well, you can see for yourself I'm no bigger than a matchstick."

"It's sure okay with me," I said.

"All right," said Luke at last. "It's a deal. Ten dollars and we'll take you to Las Vegas."

Hank opened his sack and peered inside. After a few seconds he reached in and drew out a ten-dollar bill.

"Thanks," he said, handing me the bill. "You're doing me a favor."

I was dying to have a peek into that sack. For all I knew, it could have been full of money. Whatever was in it, though, must have been pretty special to Hank, for he never once let go of it.

Before long we rounded a corner and came upon a giant brown valley. At the center of 'the valley sat a tiny town I took to be Baker. It didn't look like much from a distance and up close it didn't improve any, but we pulled off the highway anyhow and cruised down its one street looking for something to drink. We passed a tin-roofed repair shop, a general store, and a host of gas stations before Luke finally drew up at a Dairy Delite and we all got out and ordered fresh-squeezed lemonades from a fat girl in a pink checked top.

After we'd paid we took the drinks over to a little wooden table and sat down. The table looked as if it had been carved up by every kid for a hundred miles around, and there were flies working on a gob of ketchup in the middle. But the table was in the shade and that was all that mattered with me.

Hank took off his cap and ran his fingers through his stringy hair. "Been coming into Baker for ten years now, but this is the first time I've ever stopped into the Dairy Delite. Usually I just pick up my pistachios and scoot back to the mine."

"You a prospector?" asked Luke.

"Used to be," he said, "but for the last ten years I've been watching over some mines for a big company in Los Angeles. Never paid much, but then I never needed much either."

"They give you a place to live?" I asked.

"They did," said Hank, "but they're booting me out at the end of the month—abandoning the mines, they say."

"They won't let you stay?" said Luke.

Hank sighed and stared off down the road. "Nope. Told me to pack up and get out. After ten years." He looked me in the eye and shook his head. For a moment I thought he might burst out in tears. "Now, where's an old man like me going to find a place to live out the rest of his life?"

"Got any family?" asked Luke.

He took a long drink of lemonade and stared out into the desert.

I looked over at my brother and nodded. "Come on," I said. "We better get on the road."

Poor old Hank, I thought, settling in as Luke wheeled

us back onto the freeway. I wished there were some way I could help him out. But I knew that I couldn't, for I was even poorer than he was.

We rode in silence for maybe fifteen minutes while I tried to think of something to say that might cheer us all up. I finally thought of a subject that, if nothing else, made me happy.

"Say, Hank," I said. "Out here you ever get KFMB on the radio? The Padres are playing the Giants tonight, at seven-thirty."

"I wouldn't know," said Hank. "Couldn't ever afford to keep up a radio. Batteries cost too much."

I smiled. "Well, I hope we can pick up the game, because with Mark Monroe pitching for the Padres it's going to be a slaughter. And I wouldn't want to miss it for anything."

Every time we'd round a mountain now another huge, empty valley would come into view. At the end of the last of these we came upon a most amazing sight. It was a pink-and-gray plaster castle surrounded by a parking lot and topped by a huge neon sign that proclaimed it as Whiskey Pete's Casino.

We whizzed by it as if it were a desert mirage and raced on toward Las Vegas, some sixty miles distant. No doubt about it. We had come to Nevada.

4

EVERYTHING ON
THE RED

The desert kept rolling by without so much as a farm-house to break up the scenery. Finally a spot of civiliza-tion called Pop's Oasis appeared on the right. From the highway it didn't look to be much more than a few block buildings and a handful of trailers. A tall sign atop the main blockhouse advertised gambling, drinks, food, and air conditioning.

What made the place interesting was its neighbor, a state prison, complete with towers, barbed wire, and searchlights on its high gray walls.

"Seems kind of cruel putting a place like Pop's

right next to a prison, doesn't it, Hank? Looking at that sign all day must drive those convicts crazy," I said.

When Hank didn't reply, I turned around and saw that the old man had slumped over in the seat. At first I thought he might have been dead, but then I noticed his mouth moving, as if he were muttering to himself, and I knew he was only asleep. I smiled and was about to turn away when I saw something that made me gasp with surprise. His paper sack, the one he'd guarded so jealously, was lying open beside him, and a whole bunch of crumpled bills, some of them hundreds, had fallen out onto the seat.

"Luke," I whispered, "that bag of his is open. It's full of cash!"

"Really? How much?" asked Luke.

"A lot," I said. "Hundreds, maybe thousands."

Luke looked over his shoulder at Hank, then turned back to the road. "I bet he stole it. What do you think?"

"I think I better get it back in the sack before the wind blows it out the window." I clucked my tongue. "Give me a break, Luke. Does Hank look like a thief?"

Luke glanced into the rearview mirror. "Jamie, I don't know what he looks like, do you?"

I leaned over the seat, picked up the sack, and began shoving the bills back inside. "Luke, you're such an untrusting—"

"So!" snarled Hank, springing to life. Before I could move, he'd seized me by the wrist and pulled me in close. "Thought you'd steal my poke, did you?"

"I—I—I—" I stammered.

"And I thought the only snakes in this world were the kind that crawled on their bellies," he snorted.

He gave my wrist a turn and the clutch of bills fluttered out of my hand. "That all of it?" he demanded.

It wasn't easy looking into his snarling red lips and splintered teeth, but I raised up my head and fixed him with the sternest gaze I could muster. "I suggest you let go of my hand. Right now," I said. "And for your information, mister, I wasn't taking your money. I was putting it back. Saving it for you, not stealing it."

He narrowed his eyes and thought over what I'd said.

"Hank," I said, "let me go—now!"

He grunted and released my hand. Then, mumbling to himself, he peered into the sack and made as if he were counting the bills.

"I was doing you a favor," I said. "That money of yours was about to blow out the window."

"See, Jamie," said Luke, "—what did I tell you?"

I glared at Luke, then looked back at Hank. We eyed each other for a moment, like cats on a fence. Finally, Hank clenched his teeth and closed up the bag. "This here's all the money I got," he said, shaking his head. "Put yourself in my shoes. You'd be touchy too."

I rubbed my wrist and looked out at the highway rushing under the car. "You don't have to ride with us, you know."

"Listen, when I woke up, first thing I saw was a

hand holding a whole bunch of my money. Wouldn't you have done the same?''

"Yeah, maybe," I said, "but, Hank, you should know that Luke and I wouldn't—"

I felt a tap on my shoulder, and when I glanced around I saw Hank's hand, full of pistachios. "Please, let's be friends," he said. "I didn't mean no harm, believe me."

I sighed, took the nuts, and passed some on to Luke. Then I turned around and looked into Hank's sad eyes and wrinkled face. He looked as pathetic as an old dog in the rain. "Don't you trust nobody?" I asked.

"I guess I just got a little scared," said Hank. "I can't afford to lose this money."

"If you want to keep it you ought to get it out of that sack," said Luke. He cracked open a nut with his teeth and spit the shells out the window. "What's wrong? Don't you believe in banks?"

"If I was looking for a bank, I'd have gone the other way, to Barstow," he said. "This money is heading for the Firebird Hotel. I'm betting it on roulette."

I felt my jaw sag open in surprise. "Hank"—I gasped—"are you a gambler?"

He bit his lower lip, smiled, and said, "No, I ain't a gambler. Just an old fool with a sackful of money." He stared out the window for a moment, then turned back and fixed me with his pale blue eyes. "I got twelve thousand dollars in this sack, Jamie, but it ain't enough. I need twenty, and quick."

"You serious?" said Luke.

"Dead serious. Going to put it all down on the red, every last cent. If the ball lands on the black, I lose. If it hits the red, I double my money." Hank clenched his teeth. "Going to hope for the best."

"You mean hope for the red," said Luke, smiling.

We passed a sign advertising the Tropicana Hotel and Casino. Just thirty miles ahead, it said, on the Fabulous Las Vegas Strip.

"Been saving this up for ten years," he continued. "A few more years and I would have had enough to retire on. Twenty thousand, I figured, would be enough."

"You really must need that money bad," I said. "What's it for?"

He gripped the sack a little tighter and squirmed about in the seat. "It's—it's for my granddaughter. In Colorado. She needs an operation to stay alive. It'll cost twenty thousand dollars and her mother don't have it."

"But surely the hospital just wouldn't let her die," I said. "You certain they have to have the whole twenty thousand?"

"Of course I'm certain! It's my granddaughter, isn't it?"

"I can't believe something couldn't be worked out," said Luke. "Gambling's a losing proposition, Hank. It really is."

Hank glared at Luke but didn't say anything. Finally he snorted to himself, turned, and stared blankly out the window.

I felt terrible for Hank. A person shouldn't have to gamble away their life savings just because their grandchild gets sick. It didn't seem right. But maybe it was, and too bad at that.

Ten minutes later we came through a little gap in the mountains and looked out across twenty miles or so of barren, sunburnt desert to a city of glass and concrete shimmering out of the sands like a painted mirage.

"Las Vegas," said Luke. "We made it."

We dropped down from the hills, scooted through the desert for a few more miles, and finally turned off the freeway and onto the Las Vegas Strip, a wide boulevard lined with nothing but hotels, casinos, and souvenir shops. According to a big time-and-temperature sign it was 103 degrees, the kind of weather that normally drives people to air-conditioners and swimming pools, but apparently people in Las Vegas played by different rules because the sidewalks were jammed. Full of every kind of person imaginable. And I mean every single kind.

People in shiny black suits arm in arm with ladies in evening gowns, bums in torn, rumpled pants, college kids in shorts and sunglasses, families with kids and their kids with balloons. Beautiful people, ugly people, fat people and thin. Just about something of everything. But I'd say the majority of them were over sixty, overweight, and overdressed. By overdressed I mean they were wearing the kind of clothes they wouldn't have been caught dead in at home. Electric-blue shorts, neon orange socks, shirts plastered with dumb sayings. They were on vacation in Las Vegas and must have figured anything goes. And, from what I'd seen of the town so far, anything probably did.

It was definitely one weird place. Just about every hotel sign was bigger than the place it advertised. And the places they advertised were huge! Out in front of the Hacienda Hotel, for instance, was a revolving, six-story horse. A fifty-foot steel-and-neon sultan guarded the entrance to the Aladdin, giant glass palm trees framed the entrance to the Dunes, and a red-and-orange clown, easily a hundred feet tall, smiled down on Las Vegas from the lawn in front of the Circus Circus.

The whole place was like a fantasy gone berserk. We cruised slowly past one gaudy hotel after another, Caesars Palace and the Imperial Palace, the Barbary Coast and the Showboat, the Dunes, the Sands, and the El Morocco, till at last there rose up a sign that put everything that had come before it to shame. This ten-story goliath, made up of a galaxy of stars and planets and comets, loomed over a blue-mirrored place called the Firebird Hotel and Casino.

"Hey! That's it!" shouted Hank. He leaned out the window and squinted up at the Firebird's sign. "Luke, pull in."

"Hank," said Luke, "you sure you know what you're doing?"

Hank yanked his head back into the car. "Pull in that parking lot," he barked. "I want to get out."

"You're the boss," muttered Luke, and he swung the car across a lane of traffic and onto a sea of asphalt packed nearly solid with cars.

"You two coming in?" asked Hank.

"Of course," I said.

"Jamie, I don't think kids are allowed in casinos," said Luke.

I rolled my eyes. "Luke, if you want to wait in the car out here in the hot sun, that's fine with me, but I'm going in. I want to see Hank make his bet."

"They're going to kick us out, I know it. Might even put us in jail. There's gangsters here, too, Jamie, and—"

"As usual, dear brother, you worry too much," I said. "Park the car. Come on, this will be fun."

Luke muttered something to himself and pulled into a parking space not far from the entrance.

After we'd all gotten out, I gave Hank a little tap on the arm. "Nervous?"

Hank looked at his old paper bag and sighed. "Yeah, a little."

A little! The old man looked as shaky as a rookie on opening day. "You sure this is the right thing, now?"

He gave me a weak smile and replied, "I don't know if it's right, my friend, but it's what I got to do."

Just before we stepped through the Firebird's big glass doors, Hank paused and glanced once again at the sack holding his life savings.

"Last chance," I said.

He put his lips together, hard. Then, shaking his head, he pushed open the door to the Firebird Hotel and Casino. "Come on, kids. Let's go make us some money."

5

THE
FIREBIRD HOTEL
AND CASINO

Walking through the Firebird's doors was like walking into another world. Really. Vegas from the outside had just seemed strange, but inside, things became absolutely bizarre. The first thing that hit me was the air. Being air conditioned it was cool, of course, but what stunned me more was the amount of cigarette smoke it contained. If I hadn't known better, I might have looked for a fire alarm. Everybody in the place, and it was jammed, had to have been puffing away to foul the air that much. And was it ever noisy! Just about the time my nose started to settle down, I realized my ears were working overtime. *Bang! Bang! Bang!* An old lady with fat dangling under her arms and a pair of red chopsticks stuck in her hair was pounding her fist on a slot machine not three feet away,

"Give me back my nickel!" she was screaming. "I've been robbed."

Bang! Bang! Bang!

The lady next to her, feeding nickels into a machine of her own, never even glanced over. Nobody did, in fact, but maybe me and Hank and Luke. If anybody in San Diego had gone that crazy in a public place they'd soon be on their way to the jail or the nuthouse. Like my Dad. But here no one was paying this lady the slightest attention.

"Yo eleven!" came a shout from somewhere deep inside the casino.

Whang! Tika, tika, tika, tika, came the sounds of a thousand slot machines. Everywhere you turned, in fact, you saw rows of gold-and-red slot-machines. And in front of every one, often with a cup full of nickels or quarters in their hand, was a gambler, usually an old lady with a sprayed hairdo and a touch too much makeup. *Whang! tika, tika, tika....*

"Paging Mr. Clean," said someone over the Firebird's public address system. "Mr. Clean, paging Mr. Clean."

I glanced about hurriedly, looking for a bald-headed genie to answer the page.

Some of the slot machines had bells on them. And

every time one of these would go off, a pile of nickels would clatter out onto a tray.

Whang! tika tika tika RRRRRRING! Clanta clanta clank!

"Paging Mr. Clean!"

"Where's the manager? This machine's got my nickel!"

The three of us stood and gaped, frozen by the smells and the sounds and the sights, stiff as scarecrows in a cornfield.

Finally Luke said, "You sure this isn't an insane asylum? These people are nuts!"

"Crazy, maybe, but not nuts," I said. "In a way it's kind of exciting, don't you think?"

Luke tugged at his ear. "You think it's exciting to throw money away?"

"These people aren't throwing their money away," I said. "They're investing it—for a few seconds."

Even Hank had to laugh at that.

"Come on. Let's find ourselves that roulette wheel," he said, grinning.

Slowly we weaved our way deeper into the casino. On the way we passed a sign saying NO ONE UNDER 21 ALLOWED IN THE CASINO, but it didn't really register in my head. The whole place seemed so unreal to me, I couldn't imagine any kind of earthly rules applied.

Now suddenly the *whang tika tika* of the slot machines was overpowered by the frantic shouts and screams of a group of people in a large open room just to our right.

"Get 'em, Johnny. Get 'em, get 'em, get 'em!"

"Come on, six!"

"Yes!" screamed a woman.

"No!" screamed another.

We came to a halt and looked into the big room. From a distance it had sounded like a riot was breaking out. Up close I discovered it was just a bunch of people getting excited over a show on TV. Luke was quick to point out, however, that what everyone in the room was watching on a big screen TV was no ordinary show.

"It's a horse race," he said. "They got bets on it."

They must have been pretty big bets, judging by the way they were screaming and shouting. A white-haired man with a big puffy nose was rooting so hard for horse number six, I thought he was going to have a heart attack—jumping up and down, with one arm waving at the TV, his face the color of a ripe strawberry. I couldn't take my eyes off him, and when number four passed six at the wire he shook his fist at the TV and began cursing the jockey, accusing him of purposely losing.

Hank shook his head. "I never did understand horse bettors. Way I see it, anybody who'd trust their money to a stupid horse has got to be pretty dumb themselves."

"I suppose you think a roulette wheel has brains," said Luke.

"It's the few brains he's got that gets the horse into

trouble,'' said Hank. He gave Luke a short, knowing smile. ''You think I'm making a mistake, don't you?''

Luke looked away and stared off at the horse bettors. When he turned back he said, ''Gamblers are losers, Hank, and I should know. I've had to live with one all my life.''

''Dad's just had some bad luck,'' I said. ''He himself told me once that if you live on the edge long enough, you're bound to fall someday.''

''Someday? That guy's been falling since the day he was born.''

While Luke and I were discussing our father, Hank was nervously eating his way through a pile of pistachios. After a short time he wandered away, looking for a place to dump the shells. By the time we caught up with him, we were in another large room, this one dominated by three giant screen TVs and a large plastic board covered with the names of baseball teams.

''Look at that,'' I said, gesturing up at the board. ''They have the Padres listed up there.''

''What you're looking at is today's baseball schedule,'' explained Luke. ''See, it shows that the Padres are playing the Giants. Looks to me like the game is even money.''

''Even money?'' I said. ''You mean you can bet on it?''

RRRRIING! Somewhere a slot machine was paying off.

Hank soon reappeared, dusting off his hands. "Let's find us that wheel," he said.

I looked back up at the board. Davis was pitching for the Giants, Monroe for the Padres, it said.

"Luke, have you seen a wheel around—"

"Wait," I said, putting my hand on the old man's arm for emphasis. "Don't be in such a hurry, Hank."

Hank gave me a quizzical look. "What are you talking about?"

"Dad once said that the easiest way to skin a cat isn't always the best. That's what I'm talking about."

"So what's that supposed to mean?" asked Luke.

"It means maybe Hank ought to think about other ways to bet his money."

"Jamie!" said Luke.

I glared up at Luke then turned to Hank. "Hank, what do you figure the odds are on you hitting that red?"

"Fifty-fifty, I reckon." Hank took off his cap and scratched his head. "What do you figure they are?"

"I figure same as you," I said, "but I figure the Padres got a near hundred percent chance of whipping the Giants tonight."

"Jay-me, Jay-me," said Luke, as if he were talking to a three-year-old. "Hank wants to bet on roulette, not on baseball."

I shook my head and drew out my words as if talking to a two-year-old. "I know that, Luke, I know.

I'm just trying to make things a little easier for him. That's all.''

"What do you mean easier?" asked Hank.

"I'm saying that Monroe is pitching for the Padres, and there is absolutely no way he can lose. Not against the Giants.''

"Jamie, it's Hank's money," said Luke.

Hank put his hands on his hips and stared up at the board.

"You really think they can win, huh?"

"I'm positive," I said. "I've heard practically every game they've played this year.''

"Jamie, we're talking about twelve thousand dollars," said Luke.

I dismissed Luke with a wave of my hand and looked up at Hank. "I just think you'd be better off with the Padres than with the red, unless there's some reason you like that color.''

"No special reason," said Hank. "Just read about someone playing it in a book. Remember they won.''

I patted Hank on the arm and when he looked down I gave him a big fat wink. "I'm giving you inside information, Hank.''

"I gotta have twenty thousand dollars," he said.

"You do what you want," I said. "It is your money.''

Luke shook his head. "I can't believe the hospital wouldn't make some kind of a deal. Why gamble away the money you've already got?"

What a worrywart, I thought. Luke didn't seem to understand that a bet on the Padres wasn't a gamble. It was a sure thing.

Hank ignored Luke and stared off into the casino. I couldn't tell for sure, but I imagined his thoughts must have been on his granddaughter wasting away in that Colorado hospital. After a long time his eyes settled on my Padres T-shirt and he let out a giant sigh. "By golly," he said, finally allowing a little smile to play across his wrinkled face, "by golly, we'll do it. Jamie, we'll put it all on your Padres."

Then, before I could say, "Waitaminute," Hank was up at the window under the board, handing his paper sack to a droopy-eyed man in a white shirt and bow tie.

"I want to bet this on the San Diego Padres," he said. "That okay?"

"Okay with me," said the clerk, dumping the twelve thousand onto the counter. "Let's see what you got here."

The clerk began counting out the money as if old wrinkled red-lipped men gave him sacks full of cash every day. Course, for all I knew they did.

All in all there turned out to be twelve thousand one hundred and eighty-six dollars in there. He gave Hank back the hundred and eighty-six and wrote him up a blue ticket for the San Diego Padres.

"This is your receipt. Don't lose it, now," said the clerk. "And good luck, sir."

"Don't need no luck," said Hank. He slipped the receipt into one of his back pockets. "This little lady here is an expert when it comes to baseball. She's practically guaranteed I'm going to win."

I gulped, looked at the clerk, and forced out a smile. "It'll be all over by the fifth," I said.

6

THE PADRES
AND THE GIANTS

I was a fool, plain and simple. Me and my big fat mouth had talked Hank into betting his life savings on a baseball game. How stupid! If the Padres lost it would be my fault. What in the world had I been thinking of? Or, as Luke was quick to point out, had I been thinking at all?

The worst of it, said Luke, was that, thanks to me, we were now stuck in town overnight. Luke was no friend of Hank's, but even he could see it wouldn't be right to skip out on him now. Since it was convenient, we checked into the Firebird, with Hank generously footing the bill.

Our rooms were on the sixth floor, overlooking the Fabulous Las Vegas Strip. It was noisy, because of all the traffic, but kind of exciting, too, and I spent the first five minutes in the room leaning out the window watching all the crazy-looking people passing below. The room itself appeared to have been designed by a crushed-velvet salesman. The chairs, the bedspread, and even the drapes were made of the cheapest purple cloth I'd ever seen. Either they'd picked it up on sale, or someone at the Firebird was angling to win the Bad Taste Award for Hotel-Room Decoration.

I will say this, though: the beds were comfortable, the place was air conditioned, it had a radio, and the radio got KFMB.

"We're in luck," I said, after fiddling with the dial. "We'll be able to hear the game right here in the room."

After we washed up, we went back into the main part of the hotel and wandered around amid the noise and the smoke and the greed till we discovered a large cafeteria modestly named the Fabulous Firebird Buffet. It looked like a good deal—three dollars for all you could eat—and so we paid our money and went inside. The buffet was far from fabulous, but the chicken, the potatoes, and the salad were worth the price of admission and nobody complained but Hank, who said it all looked downright unhealthy.

"I'll stick to my pistachios," he said, emptying a handful onto the table. "I care too much about my body to fill it up with the poisons they're serving here."

I thought he might have been exaggerating a little. Most of the food looked safe enough to me, but I did turn down the day's dessert, a bowlful of Jell-O topped with whipped cream. But that was only because the Jell-O was the color of canned peas, and I don't eat anything that color, ever.

Once back in the room we called up Mom collect and told her we'd been delayed.

"We have to stay overnight in Las Vegas," I said. "I accidentally talked Hank into—"

"Hank! Hank who?"

"He's just this old prospector who we picked up in the desert and—"

"You picked up a hitchhiker! A hobo! Jamie! Ja ... Ja ..."

"Mom, he isn't a hobo," I said. "In fact he had more money than we did, a whole sackful of it—thousands of dollars in cash."

"A bag? Cash!" She lowered her voice to a bare whisper. "Jamie, heavens! he's a bank robber ... or—or worse. Maybe a kidnapper! Listen to me, Jamie, and listen carefully. You've got to make a run for it. Where is he now?"

"Right here," I said. "In the room we just rented."

There was a long silence at the other end and I was almost certain that Mom had fainted. "Mom! Mom!" I shouted. "Mom!"

After what seemed an eternity she came back on the phone and I was able to explain that we'd taken two separate rooms, that Hank was neither a crook nor a kidnapper and that the reason we had to stay was the bet.

"You bet how much on ... on ..."

"On the Padres," I explained. "Isn't it exciting!"

"Put Luke on the phone," she said.

Luke got on and said, "Yes, Mom.... It's okay, Mom. Yes, I know I promised ... but ... No, Mom, I won't let her out of my sight.... Yes, Mom, we'll call.... I know it's hard not to worry, I worry, too, but ... all right, the jungle, I got it. I'll be sure to tell her.... Good-bye, Mom."

Luke hung up then shook his head and gave me his standard look of exasperation. "Why did you have to tell her all that stuff? You know how she worries."

"I guess I just don't know how to lie," I said. "What about the jungle?"

Luke smiled. "Oh, the jungle. Mom says, 'Why is it dangerous to play cards in the jungle'?"

"I don't know," I said. "Hank, do you know?"

Hank shook his head.

"Because of all the cheetahs!" said Luke.

I groaned. "Mom must be awfully worried to resort to a joke like that," I said.

"If you were in her shoes you'd be worried too," said Luke. "You would be. Admit it."

I put my hands on my hips and clucked my tongue. "No, I wouldn't be," I said. "You and Mom are the worriers in the family, remember. I side with Dad, who says, and I quote, 'The only thing worrying ever gets you is wrinkles.' "

"Turn on the radio," said Luke. "I'd like to hear another voice for a while, if you don't mind."

I stuck out my tongue, then crossed to the little radio between the twin beds and tuned in KFMB. For a half hour or so we listened to music and talked about my dad. Hank laughed at all the crazy stories we told about my father and said he'd like to meet him someday.

"The things he does are funny only when you hear about them secondhand," said Luke. "Living out those stories wasn't the slightest bit fun. Believe me. I know."

"The one you should meet is my grandfather," I said. "He was a prospector in the old days. Same as you."

"Not many of us left," said Hank. "He still working?"

"Not since Grandma died," said Luke. "My mom says he spends most of his time feeling sorry for himself, and the rest of the time being sick."

"The two kind of go together, don't they?" said Hank.

"I suspect," I said.

At seven-fifteen the pregame show came on the radio and everyone got quiet. "Good evening," came the familiar voice of the Padres' announcer, Don Hart. "Tonight it's the San Diego Padres against the San Francisco Giants. For San Francisco, Mike Davis will be on the mound, and for the Padres it will be their ace,

Mark Monroe, currently the hottest pitcher in the National League.''

I gave Hank a wink. ''See what he said. Ace.''

Hank smiled and sat down in a worn, purple velvet chair near the window. He'd found some pistachios in a gift shop at the Firebird and all his pockets were bulging with nuts. He pulled out a couple of handfuls and set them down on a table beside him.

''Help yourself,'' he said. ''Oughta have something to go with the game, and these things are better than peanuts. Full of calcium, phosphorus, and not a lick of cholesterol either. Go on. Take all you want.''

''Thank you,'' I said. I picked up a handful and passed some on to Luke. Though Hank and Luke usually cracked the shells with their teeth, I preferred my fingers. Hank said he didn't mind the cracked teeth 'cause he lived out in the middle of nowhere, but having the lips and teeth of a bloodsucker would never do for me. Kids tend to notice it when you look like Dracula, and the ribbing I'd get would be something awful.

We listened to the pregame show for a while, then Hank asked, ''What did your grandpa prospect for?''

''I think he looked for uranium,'' said Luke. ''In Wyoming.''

Hank swept a pile of shells into the wastebasket and nodded his head. ''Done some uranium prospecting myself in the old days. Your grandpa ever find anything?''

''Not that I know of,'' I said. ''But he talks a lot

about a place he'd like to prospect just outside of Durango.''

"He's always talking," said Luke.

"Most old-timers usually are." Hank laughed. "But that's interesting. I've heard stories about Durango too. I'd like to talk to your granddad someday. We maybe could help each other."

"I think Grandpa needs to talk to a psychiatrist, not a prospector," said Luke. "Mom says he's real depressed these days."

Hank appeared to be awfully curious about my grandfather, but before he could ask any more questions we heard the national anthem come floating out of the radio and all of us knew that meant the game was about to begin.

For a few moments we'd forgotten about the game, but now we forgot about everything else. As the Giants were taking the field, Hank stood up and began to pace about the room nervously. I gritted my teeth and watched him sympathetically. Our ears were tuned to the radio, but I think our minds were all with that frail little girl clinging to life in that Colorado hospital.

No one scored in the first two innings, but in the top of the third the Padres struck for two runs on a pair of back-to-back doubles and a single. When the inning was over, Hank finally sat down, and I saw his old eyes begin to sparkle. I was feeling a little better myself. "You see?" I said. "No sweat."

Hank could barely contain himself. "They're whupping 'em good, ain't they?"

"They're ahead," I said. But, knowing baseball like I did, I knew that two runs didn't amount to diddley. And in the fifth, when the Giants' Dusty Carter smashed his fourteenth homer over the right-field wall, cutting the Padres' lead to one, it suddenly didn't seem like a whupping at all.

The Giants didn't get any more runs in the fifth, but they'd tightened things up enough to get Hank back up on his feet and pacing. We were all a little nervous, of course. My mouth felt dry as cotton. I suspected that Luke's did, too, what with all the times he went into the bathroom for a glass of water. We all could have used a joke or two to lighten things up. Where was Mom now that we needed her?

The innings seemed to drag by, every pitch took forever, every out an eternity. No one scored in the sixth or the seventh and when Monroe struck out the side in the bottom of the eighth I began to think the Padres just might have it after all.

"Three outs to go," I said. "Looks like we got it."

"Three more outs is three more outs," Hank said. "Lots can happen." He paused and added, "I'm not counting my money till it's all over." Then, lowering his head, he went back to wearing down the carpet.

His pacing may have done some good, because the Padres came up with another run in the top of the ninth, stretching their lead to three to one.

Going into the bottom of the ninth I was beginning to feel like just about the smartest thing on earth. Why, I was on the verge of making more money for Hank in three hours than lots of folks made in a year. Yes, sir, I was feeling like some pretty hot stuff. So, when Monroe got two quick strikes on the Giants' leadoff batter, Andy Cordero, I didn't feel the least bit shy about bragging some.

"What'd I tell you, Hank, what'd I tell you. Aren't those Padres something, though? Why, Hank I do believe they could've beaten—"

I never did get to finish up what I was saying, because right in the middle of all my blathering Cordero hit the ball over the center-field fence and suddenly it was a one-run ball game again.

Monroe got the next batter to pop up for the first out, but the next man hit a single and like a shifting wind you could feel the momentum begin to swing toward the Giants.

Luke began nervously tugging at his ear and Hank said, "Monroe's in trouble." He spit another pistachio shell into the wastebasket. "Us too."

"Padres are still leading," said Luke. "Let's not forget that."

But forget it we did when moments later Tony Roberts lined a fastball into the corner for a triple and the tying run came in to score.

I was stunned. Though not near so as Hank. The old man staggered over to the velvet chair and collapsed into it as if he'd had the wind knocked out of him. For a moment or two I thought he was going to have a heart attack and up and die on us. It wouldn't have surprised me, that's for sure. My own heart was going pretty good itself.

"I—I—I don't believe it," Hank finally said. "The winning run is on third. There's only one out." His eyes looked round as silver dollars. "I'm finished, finished, plain and simple."

"Game's not over," said Luke, still trying to look on the bright side. "The Giants haven't won yet."

That was true enough, but matters had looked better. However, when the Padres manager sent to the bullpen for Binky Homan to take over the pitching, I felt my hopes pick up some.

"If anyone can pitch our boys out of trouble, it's Binky," I said. "There isn't a better reliever in the majors."

Hank gave me a kind of half nod and closed his eyes. He didn't particularly seem like a praying kind of man, but that very well may be what he was doing.

"Everything I worked for, ten years," I heard him mutter.

I didn't mind telling you, those words made me feel lower than a penny in a well bottom. I wanted to kick myself for ever opening my mouth about the Padres. No wonder folks hated gambling so much. I vowed right then and there I'd never wager another cent as long as I lived.

Homan finished his warm-up tosses and the Giants' shortstop, Mike Malaga, stepped to the plate with one out and the winning run on third. Even now it's hard for me to tell you what happened next. So I'll leave the description to Don Hart. Here's the way he called it on the radio:

"Stepping to the plate to face Binky Homan is young Mike Malaga. Mike's one for four today, up now with a chance to drive in Roberts, the winning run at third."

I remember crossing my fingers.

"Homan winds and pitches. Low, ball one."

Hank reached into his back pocket and drew out the slip of paper representing his bet.

"Swing and a miss! Strike one on a sizzling fastball."

"Come on, Binky," said Luke softly.

Hank kept his eyes down, fiddling with the paper as if to take his mind off of what was happening on the radio.

"Homan checks the runner at third. Now he sets, winds, and delivers the pitch to Malaga who SWINGS! and lifts a fly ball to the left. Kleinford is back to make the catch, but Roberts is tagging at third. This could be the ball game unless Kleinford gets off a strike to the plate!"

I shut my eyes.

"Here comes Roberts. He's pumping for home. Look out! Here comes the throw from Kleinford. It's gonna be close. Hold on ... Nellie! Roberts slides ... Heeeeee's safe! And the San Francisco Giants, picking up three runs here in the ninth, have won the game by the score of four to three. We'll be back with all the stats in just a moment. From Candlestick Park this has been Padres base—''

I reached over and clicked off the radio. I couldn't recall the last time I'd felt so sick.

"Ah, Hank," I said. "I'm sorry. I'm real sorry."

Hank gave me a long, vacant look. Then, unfolding himself from the chair, he got to his feet and shook his head.

"I don't know what to say," I said.

"I'm sorry," said Luke.

Hank gave out a pathetic groan, crumpled up his ticket, and tossed it into the trash, where it settled down on a pile of red pistachio shells. The ticket was garbage now, but two minutes before it had been worth twelve thousand dollars, and almost more than twenty.

Hank shuffled to the door, shaking his head.

"You can stay if you want," I said.

Without answering, or turning back, Hank opened the door and disappeared into the hallway.

I turned to Luke.

"What are we going to do?" I asked.

"Call Mom for gas money," he replied.

7

TAKING IT TO THE TOP

Getting to sleep that night was no easy task. It seemed that every time I'd shut my eyes I'd start thinking about Hank, or his granddaughter, or even worse yet, Tony Roberts streaking home with the winning run for San Francisco. Poor Hank. His granddaughter was maybe going to die now, and all because of me and my big trap.

One thing I knew for sure, I couldn't let Hank go home broke. "Any fool can get himself into trouble. The real trick, sweet pea, is getting out of it." That's what Dad used to say.

Lying there in the bed that night I must have run

through a million schemes. I thought of everything from selling the car to raise money for gambling to robbing a bank.

Gambling was out. I'd learned the hard way that you couldn't make any money picking baseball games. And bank robbing wouldn't do either. Too dangerous. I had a definite fear of guns, particularly ones pointed my way.

As I said, I couldn't get to sleep, and that may have been for the best, because at about two in the morning I remembered something that made me think I had a chance to get Hank's money back after all. That something I remembered was a sign I'd seen just inside the Firebird Hotel, a sign that said: NO ONE UNDER 21 ALLOWED IN THE CASINO.

The meaning of that sign seemed clear enough: no minor could go into a casino and gamble. Yet that's just what I'd done, gone into the casino and made a bet. Oh, maybe I hadn't actually put the money down on the counter, but if it hadn't been for me, that bet never would have been made. Never. No doubt about it. I'd broken the law. More important, the Firebird had broken the law, too, by taking the bet. Lying there in bed that night I somehow talked myself into believing that the Firebird Hotel and Casino owed us a refund, and all I'd have to do to collect was stop by the manager's office and explain things in a rational way.

I must have finally fallen asleep, because the next thing I knew it was nine in the morning and the room was full of sunshine. I got up quietly, put on the dress I'd packed back in San Diego, and tiptoed to the door.

"Jamie!" said Luke. I turned around and saw him up on one elbow. "Jamie, where are you going?"

"Nowhere," I said hastily. "Out."

"Nowhere! I know better than that, Jamie Pluf-phanger. You're wearing a dress. Now, where are you going?"

I opened the door and smiled sweetly. "Luke, did I ever tell you that you worry too much? Now, go on, do us both a favor and go back to sleep."

"Jamie!" he shouted as I closed the door. "Don't do anything stupid ... please!"

I closed the door behind me and turned around only to find myself in a head-on collision with a stout middle-aged lady in a white starched uniform. Her arms were full of folded towels, and I bounced off her as if she'd been a giant rubber ball.

"I'm—I'm sorry," I said. "I guess I wasn't paying attention."

"I guess you weren't," she said angrily.

I forced a smile and straightened my dress. "Have a nice day," I said, then hurried off down the hallway and caught the elevator to the lobby.

When the doors opened on the first floor, the Fire-bird said hello with a blast of cigarette smoke and the *tika tika clang* of a thousand distant slot machines. An army of bald, loudmouth backslappers wearing name tags from the Asphalt Wholesalers Convention had filled the lobby, and I had to weave my way through a forest of potbellies to get to the manager's office, located just behind the Firebird's main registration desk. In back of the counter, sorting through a pile of room keys, I spotted a stick-thin woman in a Firebird uniform. Her hair, pulled back in a bun, was streaked with gray.

I drew in a deep breath, straightened out my dress, and stepped bravely to the counter.

"Excuse me, ma'am," I said. "Is the manager in?"

The lady looked up and gave me a sweet smile. "Manager? You sure I can't help you with something, young lady?"

"No, ma'am," I said firmly. "Only the manager can help me."

And I meant it too. My father used to say, "When you have a problem with the king, you gotta go to the castle." And that's just where I intended to go. Right to the top.

The lady smiled again, but I could tell she was forcing it this time. "The manager's a busy man. But I'll tell you what. Send your mommy over here and let me talk to her. Whatever the problem is, I'm sure we can work it out."

Mommy! I shook my head and rolled my eyes. Who did the bat think she was talking to? Remembering something my Dad once said in a restaurant, I put my hands on the counter and looked her squarely in the eye.

"My mommy isn't here right now," I said sarcastically. "And neither is my daddy, which happens, by the way, to be very lucky for you."

"Oh, it does, does it?"

"For your information, Miss Smarty-pants, my father owns half this hotel." I pointed to the door marked MANAGER. "Now, for the very last time, would you get him for me?"

I wouldn't say my little speech exactly convinced her I was someone important, but I do believe it planted a few doubts in her head.

She sighed and put down her pen. "What's your father's name, little girl?"

"Don't call me little girl!" I said. "Call me the manager." I put my hands on my hips and gave her the meanest look I could muster. "You do as I say or you're going to find yourself out of work."

You can imagine how well that went over.

"Listen, sweetheart," she hissed, "if you don't quit pestering me right now, I'm apt to come out from behind this counter and give you a sound spanking."

"Just get me the manager," I shouted. "Didn't you hear me say it was important? What's wrong? You deaf?"

"Don't you raise your voice to me!" she shouted back.

"Then stop screaming!" I screamed.

We went back and forth like that for maybe a minute or two, and might have gone on longer had not we been interrupted by someone with the deepest voice I'd ever heard.

''Miss Lang, what seems to be the trouble here?''

A short, bald fellow with the stub of a cigar clamped between his teeth was standing next to the open door to the manager's office.

''Well?'' he said in that bullfrog voice of his.

Miss Lang shut her eyes for a moment to compose herself. Then, gesturing across the counter, she said, ''Mr. Bardsley, this—this girl here has been pestering me to see Mr. Henniman. When I told her he was busy, she began threatening me.''

Mr. Bardsley took the cigar out of his mouth and studied me from afar. Convinced I wasn't dangerous, he finally sauntered over to the counter, leaned over, and gave me a big wink.

''Listen, honey, Mr. Henniman is kind of busy right now, but I'm his assistant. Why don't you tell me your problem and I bet I can fix it for you lickety quick.''

''I'm sorry, sir,'' I said, ''but like I told this lady here, only the manager can help me.'' I glanced about and lowered my voice. ''It's about something illegal going on here at the Firebird.''

He raised a single eyebrow. ''Illegal, you say?''

''It'll only take a minute to say my piece,'' I said. ''I promise.''

Mr. Bardsley considered for a moment, then motioned to me with his cigar to come around the side. ''I believe Mr. Henniman can spare some time for a pretty little lady like you,'' he said. ''Come on back.''

Miss Lang gave me a dirty look and then opened up

a little side door. I came around and followed Mr. Bardsley into the manager's office.

At first glance I thought the office was empty. But then I saw a gray-haired man in a shiny blue suit stretched out on a green sofa in the corner and took him to be the manager, which is just who he turned out to be.

"Bill," croaked Mr. Bardsley, "this is uh . . . uh . . ."

"Jamie," I said. "Jamie Plufphanger."

"Miss Plufphanger was telling me she has information on some sort of illegal activity going on here at the Firebird."

Mr. Henniman smiled and slowly got to his feet. As he rose up into the light, I noticed his eyes were so sunk into his head they looked like lumps of coal. He had about as spooky a face as I'd ever run into. Though it wasn't easy, I tried not to stare.

"Just what kind of illegal activity are we talking about, Miss Plufphanger?" asked Mr. Henniman.

"Well, sir," I said, "a minor has been gambling here at the Firebird. That's illegal, isn't it?"

Mr. Henniman smiled again and gave me a grandfatherly pat on the shoulder. "Are you going to tell me your parents let you pull the handle of a slot machine and now you're feeling guilty about it?"

I looked at Mr. Bardsley, then lowered my voice. "It's worse than that," I said. "I'm talking about a bet on a baseball game that was made yesterday in your casino." I paused for a little dramatic impact, then added, "A bet for twelve thousand dollars."

He looked over at Bardsley, then back at me. "One of our clerks took a bet that size from a minor?"

"From me," I said.

He gave me a quizzical look. "From you?"

"Well, it wasn't me precisely, but it might as well have been," I said. "I was standing right there when it was made. And if it hadn't been for my advice my friend never would have put it down."

Mr. Henniman shook his head. "Yes, so?"

I bit my lip and tried my best to look Henniman in the eye. "I thought that, well, maybe my friend should get his twelve thousand dollars back," I said. "Since it was done illegally I figure it wasn't a bet at all."

"I don't know how you figure that," said Mr. Henniman. "I take it your friend lost, right?"

I lowered my head and smoothed down my dress. "Mr. Henniman," I said, looking up, "my friend desperately needs that money. His granddaughter is dying and needs an operation and—and, well I don't know what's going to happen."

Henniman shrugged his shoulders, shook his head, and gave me another of those grandfatherly pats. "Jamie," he said, "did you get a good look at our casino? Did you see all those chandeliers and big thick carpets? The girls giving out the free drinks and those giant TVs?"

"Yes, sure," I said.

"Well, we didn't exactly get all that stuff by returning the money people lost at our tables. We run a money-making business here, Jamie, and a pretty good one at that. Your friend took a chance and he lost. I'm sorry about his granddaughter, but there's nothing I can do about it."

"Mr. Henniman," I said, "you don't understand. If you don't return my friend's money I'm going to the police. I'll tell them everything. That you took a bet from a minor."

"You already told me you didn't actually make that bet," said Mr. Henniman.

"Same thing," I said.

Suddenly I felt Mr. Bardsley's hand on my shoulder. "Time's up," he said in that bullfrog voice of his. "Mr. Henniman's got a busy schedule, but we do want to thank you for stopping by."

"I'm not kidding," I said. I tore his hand away from my shoulder. "I'm not afraid to go to the cops."

"Go, go to the police," said Mr. Henniman. "But you'll be wasting your time." Those spooky eyes of his narrowed. "Now get out of here. I don't like being threatened—by anyone."

"Come along," growled Bardsley.

I felt my face go red with anger. "You'll be sorry, Mr. Henniman. You'll see."

Henniman nodded to Bardsley and the assistant manager took me tightly by the arm and began marching me to the door.

"Good day, Miss Plufphanger," said Mr. Henniman.

Remembering something my dad once said under similar circumstances, I turned and shouted to Mr. Henniman over my shoulder. "You're going to hear from my attorney!"

Bardsley marched me through the door, past Miss Lang, and out through the little gate. "Don't be bothering us no more," he said, punctuating his remark with a little push.

Miss Lang gave me a cheery little wave. "Have a nice day, dear," she said.

I curled my lip and tried my best to snarl in reply, but I'm afraid I didn't end up looking very scary. That's probably because I'd started to cry.

Things certainly had not gone according to plan.

8

I GET
SURPRISED

Ten o'clock in the morning and my day was already
ruined. There was only one thing I could do. The same
thing I did every morning. Get the newspaper. There
was bound to be something in it to cheer me up. Anyway, the thought of returning to that hotel room was
something I couldn't bear. I needed time to walk and to
think and to read. So I set out to find myself the
morning paper.

I remembered seeing a newsstand at the Firebird,
but I wasn't about to give that place another cent. So, I
went out onto the street and headed up the sidewalk

figuring I'd come across a market or newspaper rack soon enough.

Soon enough came almost a half hour later. I guess gamblers aren't interested in the news, because by the time I found myself a copy of the *Los Angeles Times* at a little market next to the Castaways Hotel, I bet I'd walked over a mile in the hot sun.

There were only two people in the market when I walked in, but they were making enough racket for a hundred. The clerk was a big red-faced fellow with tiny round glasses. When I came in he was carrying on something awful with a skinny unshaven man wearing a dirty T-shirt that said: MY GRANDPARENTS WENT TO LAS VEGAS AND ALL THEY BROUGHT BACK WAS THIS LOUSY T-SHIRT. It looked like something he might have found in the street.

From what I could gather the clerk was trying to persuade the man that the Pittsburgh Steelers didn't have a chance to win the Super Bowl the coming year.

"Bud! Bud! Bud!" said the man in the T-shirt. "I got inside information. Don't be a fool. Front me the money and we'll both be rich."

"Look at yourself, Grady. There's the fool. Every cent you've ever had you've lost on stupid bets. Go on, get out. I'm tired of you and your begging."

"So I ran into a streak of bad luck. Who hasn't? Come on. All I need is a thousand bucks and—"

The clerk shook his head wearily. "Not today, Grady, please. Do me a favor. Go home and get some sleep."

"You'll regret this, Bud," said Grady. He wagged a finger in the clerk's face. "Some friend!"

"Get out," said the clerk coldly.

"When I'm ready, I will," said Grady.

"Git!" yelled Bud. "Now! Move!"

Bud's face was so red, I thought it would burst. I didn't know what was going to happen next, but I wouldn't have been surprised if one of them had pulled out a gun and started shooting. Bud looked that mad. And Grady looked that crazy.

I had a feeling it wasn't the best time to pay for the paper, so I hung back by the door and waited for the shouting to die down. While I dawdled about I opened the *Times* and turned to the sports section. There was a big story about the Dodgers on the front page, but I didn't find anything about the Padres till I got to page three, and what I found there very nearly laid me out cold.

PADRES VICTORS IN EXTRA INNINGS 4–3

I felt myself gasp, then looked up at the date to make sure I hadn't picked up last week's paper. I hadn't.

PADRES VICTORS IN EXTRA INNINGS 4–3

I read it again but still didn't believe it.

Up at the counter the fight raged on, but the sound had faded away. I shook my head and looked back at the headline.

PADRES VICTORS IN EXTRA INNINGS 4–3

I looked around to make sure no one was playing a joke on me and started reading the words lined up below the headline. This is the way it started:

Tony Roberts, tagging too early on a fly ball off the bat of Mike Malaga, was called out at third after coming across home plate with what had appeared to be the winning run in the bottom of the ninth last night in San Francisco. Binky Homan, pitching in relief of starter Mark Monroe, then went on to get Scott Herbert to ground out, retiring the side. The Padres, off a double by Terry Lacross and a single by Angel Montoya, scored what proved to be the winning run in the top of the tenth.

By the time I got to the bottom of the story my heart was going so fast, I was afraid I might pass out.

"He tagged too early," I whispered to myself. "A runner can't leave third till after the ball is caught. They must have thrown him out at third after he'd crossed home plate—and after we'd turned off the radio!"

Without thinking I threw down the paper and let out a whoop. "Whoooo-eeeee! We won!"

I started to dance a little jig right there by the door when suddenly I remembered where I was. Glancing up nervously I caught sight of Bud and Grady staring at me, dumbstruck. The fat clerk's mouth had flopped open like a tailgate on a pickup truck and it was a moment before he could collect himself. He looked at the paper lying at my feet and said, "Can I help you, young lady?"

The other fellow, Grady, scratched his belly and gave me a little smile. "What'd you win?"

"Baseball game," I said. I bent down and gathered up the paper and marched to the counter. "Look at this."

Spreading the paper out on the counter I suddenly found myself spilling out everything that had happened the last two days. That these men were perfect strangers and maybe didn't give a hoot about what I was saying never entered my mind once. I was so excited, I just couldn't stop yakking.

It wasn't till I was done that I realized the two of them were paying me a heap of attention.

"Isn't that something," said Bud, the clerk. "And I thought I'd heard every gambling story in this town. You're not pulling our legs, are you?"

"Think I could make up something like that?" I said. "It's the truth, all right. Sure is."

"Isn't that something," said Bud again.

"You really got over twenty thousand coming to you?" asked Grady. His breath smelled like a combination of stale pizza and coffee. "Could I see the ticket?"

"It's back at the Firebird," I said.

The clerk gave Grady a murderous look, then turned

to me and wagged a finger in my face. "Now, listen here, young lady. If I were you I'd get that ticket and put it away where it's safe. Twenty thousand dollars is a lot of cabbage, even in this town. There's no telling what someone might do to get their hands on that kind of cash."

Grady showed me his teeth. "You say you're staying at the Firebird?"

I looked up at him with sudden alarm and stammered out a hasty reply. "Ummmm .. was staying there. We just moved."

Grady tried to reply, but Bud cut him off.

"Get out of here, Grady. Go on. And I don't want to see you in here again. That clear?"

"I wouldn't come in here again if you paid me a thousand bucks," he said, heading for the door. "Not even for a million."

"Who are you kidding, Grady, you'd be back for ten cents," said Bud. Then, turning his attention to me, he said, "And you'd better be getting along, too, young lady. Make sure that ticket is safe."

"Yes, sir, I will, sir," I said, paying for the paper.

When I got outside Grady was leaning up against a car, squinting into the sun.

"You wouldn't be interested in doubling that money of yours, would you?" he said. His brown matted hair didn't look like it had been washed in a week. "I know just the team we can put it on."

"Thanks," I said, "but no thanks. I'm done betting."

"If you change your mind, I'll be around," he said. "The name's Grady."

I hurried away without replying. My mind now was on one thing, and one thing only—the ticket. I couldn't be certain, but I thought I remembered Hank throwing it into the wastebasket, hardly a fitting place for more than twenty thousand dollars. Within fifteen minutes I planned to have that ticket back in Hank's hands. I couldn't help but laugh out loud. Wasn't he in for a surprise.

9

THE PRICE
OF A CLEAN ROOM

Ever seen the way a ballplayer runs around the bases after hitting a game-winning home run? Clapping his hands, a grin on his face and a spring in his step. Well, that's the way I hustled back to the Firebird. You should have seen me go. I was so excited, I practically flew.

Hurrying down the hallway toward our room, winding my way past the cleaning ladies making their morning rounds, I rehearsed in my mind how I'd break the good news to Luke and Hank. I was really torn between putting 'em on some and coming right out with it the second I walked through the door.

These thoughts were still skipping through my head as I put the key into the lock and opened the door to the room. Well, you can imagine my surprise then when I discovered that no one was in the room. Worse yet, the place had been cleaned spotless. And even our suitcase was missing.

"Luke?" I called. But already by then I'd seen enough to know he'd been gone for some time.

Then, suddenly, a terrible feeling gripped at my throat. The wastebasket! I gulped, looked down, and beheld my horrified face staring back at me from the polished silver bottom of the basket. It was as empty as a dry hole.

I looked about the room in desperation and called for my brother again. "Luke!"

A sudden thought hit me. Maybe I was in the wrong room! I dashed outside, looked up at the room number, and my heart sank again. I ran next door. Maybe Luke was with Hank, and maybe he'd rescued the ticket. I pounded the door with both fists.

"Hank. Let me in!"

It wasn't long before Hank opened the door. His eyes were all red and sunk into his head and his white hair was sticking up in back like a wispy feather. Beyond him I could see Luke sitting on the edge of the bed.

"Luke!" I said, busting past Hank. "Why aren't you in our room? Where's Hank's ticket?"

"Ticket? In the trash, I suppose." Our suitcase was on the floor by the window. Luke nodded toward it, then said, "I checked us out of the room. I was worried if you didn't get back soon, we'd have to pay for an extra day."

"Luke!" I screeched. I shook both fists in his face. "You idiot. You stupid fool. They've cleaned the room!"

Luke pulled back his head and eyed me with astonishment. "Jamie, what's gotten into you?"

"Worried about the hotel checkout time? How could you be so lame?"

"Lame? You got thirty dollars to pay for another day, Miss Penniless?"

"That's not the point, dear brother. The point is that if you hadn't been such a worrywart, then Hank here would now have more than twenty thousand dollars. Twenty thousand." I threw up my arms. "Oh! You idiot!"

Hank was still holding the door. "What are you talking about, Jamie?"

I threw the paper down on the bed. "The Padres won that game last night. Roberts tagged too early. He was out and the Padres went on to take the game in extra innings. It's all there in the *Times*."

He gave me a sideways glance and raised an eyebrow. "You're kidding?"

"I'm definitely not kidding. Look at the paper."

I plopped down on the bed and glared at Luke while Hank hunted up the story, read it to himself, then out loud. A smile turned to a grin, turned to a laugh, and finally a shout.

"Ah, yes! Yes! Yes!" he said, slapping the paper over and over with the back of his hand. His eyes were sparkling again. "It's got to be either a miracle or a dream. Luke!" he cried, gesturing to my brother. "Get on over here and pinch me."

Luke, smiling, bounced over and gave Hank a little pinch on the arm.

"It ain't a dream!" he said. "No, sir, it ain't no dream."

I shook my head sadly and stared down at the open paper. "Fellows," I said softly, "the Padres may have won, but not us. We don't have the ticket, remember?"

"Hank, this is a miracle," said Luke, not paying me the slightest mind.

I whistled for attention. "Hey! Hey! Didn't you just hear me? I said we don't have the ticket."

Luke spun around and grabbed me by the shoulders. "Jamie," he said, giving me a little shake, "would you get hold of yourself for a minute? That ticket isn't lost. It's gotta be somewhere. All we got to do is track it down." He turned to Hank again. "Man, this is great. Come on, let's go find us that money."

It wasn't easy for me to confess, but Luke was right. I hadn't been thinking straight. I followed Luke and Hank into the hall. By the time I'd caught up with them, they were busy questioning one of the cleaning ladies, a hawk-nosed woman with bright orange fingernails.

"Check with Doris," I heard her say. "She mighta

been the one." She pointed to a stout woman down the hall and we headed off before the woman could lower her arm.

When we got up close to Doris, I realized she was the woman I'd run into earlier. At first I was worried she might recognize me, but she didn't pay me the slightest mind. That's because the sight of Hank positively stunned her. The way she stepped back, mouth open, she must have thought Dracula was on the prowl.

Luke snapped her back to reality. "Excuse me, ma'am. Did you clean out room six eighteen this morning?"

She looked at Luke, then back at Hank, and gathered herself together. "Yeah ... yeah," she said. "Six eighteen. That's one of my rooms."

"The stuff that was in the wastebasket," I said. "Do you still have it?"

She shook her head. "It's out in the Dumpster, the big one by the pool. What's wrong? Lose something important?"

"Real important," I said. "A slip of paper."

"Think anybody would mind if we poked around that Dumpster?" asked Luke.

"Don't matter none to me, but I think you're going to be wasting your time," she said.

"Why's that?" I asked.

She gave Hank a cautious look, making sure he wasn't about to leap at her throat, then said, "You folks know how much trash a hotel this size churns out in a day?" She paused a beat, then answered her own question. "Tons and tons and tons of it. Find a slip of paper in that giant Dumpster? Believe me, you'd sooner find a nickel buried at the bottom of the sea."

10

KNEE DEEP IN
TRASH

The Dumpster was behind the casino, and to reach it we
had to cross the hotel's parking lot. It was blinding hot
and we stepped along quickly, as if the asphalt beneath
our feet was ablaze, which it practically was.

"I hope the weather is better in Utah," said Luke.
He glanced up at the sun. "If not, it's going to be
miserable."

"No more miserable than being around Grandpa,"
I said. "If he's as bad off as Mom says, St. George is
going to be one gloomy time."

"Ain't nothing worse than a case of lonesomes,"

said Hank. He put a pistachio into his red mouth and cracked it open. "I've had a touch of 'em myself from time to time."

I bet he had, I thought. Honestly, living out in the middle of the desert with only snakes and lizards for friends would be enough to give anyone the blues.

The Dumpster wasn't hard to find. Doris had said it was huge, and she hadn't been kidding. It was absolutely gigantic, a regular Dumpster Godzilla, easily ten feet tall and nearly forty feet long. It sat not far from a chain link fence guarding the Firebird's nearly deserted pool, and when we first came alongside all we could do was stand before it and stare up at it in awe, as if it were a famous monument or statue. But then Hank found some steps welded onto the side and he climbed up and peeked over the top.

"What's it look like, Hank?" asked Luke.

"Like a lot of trash," said Hank, over his shoulder. "It's a real mess."

"Does it look hopeless?" I asked.

"Hopeless was last night," he answered. "Anything's possible now. Come on up and let's have a go at it."

Luke and I scaled the ladder and dropped down into the Dumpster. The thing was about half full. Aside from a few loose cans most everything was packed in big clear plastic trash bags.

Walking around in there was a little like moving about inside one of those Moon Walk tents they have at the fair, you know the ones, where they blow up a big air mattress, then let a bunch of kids bounce around inside till their legs give out. It was kind of like that.

"I figure the bag holding the ticket can't be buried too deep," said Hank. "We'll start at one end and work our way to the other."

Soon the three of us were knee deep in garbage. Luckily the kitchen must have used another Dumpster, because the sacks were almost entirely full of paper. That's not to say we didn't run across some banana peels, apple cores, or other bits of food, but mostly it was paper. I don't think we could have stood it any other way. In that heat a load of rotting food would have stunk so bad, we'd have needed gas masks.

One by one we'd rip open the bags, empty them out, and then paw our way through the contents. Hunting for that little slip of paper was no easy chore, believe me. You couldn't pass anything by for fear you'd miss the ticket. Of course, the heat didn't make things any more pleasant. Metal on three sides and the noonday sun above made that Dumpster like an oven. I never would have believed I could sweat so much.

And the heat wasn't the only problem either. Every once in a while a sack of garbage would come sailing over the top and land *ker-plop* in the Dumpster. A couple of times I almost got hit by one of those surprise trash bombs. I tried to keep alert to any incoming missiles, and prayed no one would decide to toss out a load of bricks that day. I shuddered at the thought of my

friends back at school reading how I'd died. JAMIE
PLUFPHANGER KILLED IN THE GARBAGE, it'd say. The
embarrassment! I'd positively die.

Figuring the Firebird might have rules about pok-
ing through the garbage, we kept ourselves hid. Only
once, after a particularly big load of bags was hurled
into the Dumpster, did Luke look out.

"See anyone?" asked Hank.

"No one to speak of," he said. "There's a bum
lying over in the shade of one of the buildings, but I
think he's asleep or passed out. Anyway, if he hears us I
doubt if he'll be running for the cops."

You'd be amazed at the things people throw away.
Aside from the usual stuff like newspapers, candy wrap-
pers, old socks, coat hangers, cans of shaving cream, and
useless airplane tickets, I ran across a whole bunch of
valuable things. Change, for one: pennies, nickels, and
even some dimes showed up more often than you might
think. All in all I bet I found close to three dollars.
Then there was the jewelry, junky stuff mostly, but
perfectly good anyhow. We also found a ton of belts,
three or four dolls, and two radios. And, of course, we
ran across our share of betting tickets, all losers. In the
beginning the sight of one of those blue betting cards
would get me so excited I'd start shouting: "I found it!
I found it!" But I was disappointed so many times I
was soon barely giving them a second look.

Naturally the hunt was great fun at first and there
was a lot of laughing and joking and talking about the

stuff that we found. But, as the sun rose higher, and the afternoon wore on, the talking slowed and finally stopped altogether.

Once, though, I remember Hank straightening up, wiping the sweat from his forehead with the back of his hand, and saying something I think had been on his mind a long time.

"I don't think your grandpa needs anyone to take care of him," he said slowly. "What I think he needs is someone to talk to."

"Could be," I said.

"And not just anyone to talk to either," he went on. "Some old lady that knows nothing but nursing couldn't cheer up an old prospector like your grandpa. He needs someone that understands him."

"I don't doubt you're right about that," I said.

"He just needs a friend," said Hank. Then, nodding as if in agreement with himself, he went back to work.

After a couple of hours we stopped to rest. Flopped down in a corner the three of us must have looked like worn rag dolls. A little breeze had suddenly sprung up, and from where we sat I could see a line of bright puffy clouds skidding over the distant mountains. Tomorrow was likely to be cloudy and cooler, but it was small comfort for those of us still frying in the sun.

I'd worked up a bit of an appetite, and when Hank offered me and Luke some pistachios, I took them gladly. For a while we just sat in silence, eating nuts and spitting shells, and watching a carpet of empty red pistachios spread out in front of us.

"Afore long I reckon someone's going to come haul this Dumpster away," said Hank. "And that'll be the end of that."

A half dozen trash bags suddenly came rising up over the lip of the Dumpster and crashed down at our feet.

"The worst of it is that they're gaining on us," said Luke. He spit out a mouthful of. shells. "You know, mucking around in trash on a hot day is not the smartest thing we can be doing. Germs just breed in this stuff. Ever hear of a staph infection? Or dengue fever? Bubonic plague? We're open to all kinds of terrible, horrible things. I think we better start considering our health, while we still got it. Face it. This is hopeless."

I glared at Luke. I would have liked to have yelled, *Quitter!* But I couldn't, because I had to admit he may have been right. It did look hopeless. *Kerplop!* Another three bags came arching over the top of the Dumpster and fell at our feet, sending a shower of pistachio shells flying into the air.

I stared at the shells and sighed, once, twice, three times. But then, before I could sigh once more, a sudden thought leapt into my head and I found myself leaping, too, right up onto my feet.

"Of course!" I exclaimed, clapping a hand to my forehead. "Why didn't we think of it before!"

"Think of what?" asked Luke.

"The pistachios!" I said. "That's how we can find the ticket."

"Pistachios?" said Hank.

"Of course! Of course!" I said, high-stepping my way through the trash till I was standing before my fellow trash-pickers. "Don't you see? We've been going about this all wrong. Instead of looking for that tiny little slip of paper, we should be looking for the rest of the stuff that was in the basket. We find that, we find the ticket."

You could almost see the light blink on in Luke's head, Hank's too. "Jamie," said Luke. "You're right."

"The pistachios!" said Hank.

"The pistachio shells!" we all shouted together.

I kicked myself for not having thought of it earlier. Why the sun must have fried my brain. It was so simple. Aside from the ticket, that wastebasket had been chock full of red pistachio shells. It figured that if we shook those clear plastic bags some of the shells were bound to filter down to the bottom.

As you might well imagine, my idea gave us all a new burst of energy. In no time we were once again plowing our way through the Firebird's garbage, shaking the bags and looking for shells. The hunt was fun once again, and I even heard Hank whistling. Within fifteen minutes we'd surveyed one whole end of the Dumpster and were working our way toward the middle when Luke let out a yell that brought us running.

"Pa—pa—pistachios!" he stammered. "Got 'em!"

I'd never seen a garbage bag held so high or so proudly. It was the one all right. The pile of shells visible through the plastic was proof enough of that. For a moment or two we all just stood and stared and grinned. Finally Hank said, "Open 'er up!"

Then we were on our hands and knees again, clawing through the paper, till at last I caught sight of a patch of blue, reached underneath an empty can of Coke, and pulled out our bet on the San Diego Padres. "I have it! I have it!" I screeched.

I almost felt as if I was going to faint. Luke, grinning, took the ticket and passed it to Hank, who received it into his hands as if it were an ancient, fragile document. He read it to himself, then looked up and shook his head with wonder.

"We found it," he said softly. He looked at me and I saw his eyes fill with tears. "You kids found it." Then, suddenly, the old man leaned over and gave me a kiss on the cheek. For a moment he drew back, looking a little embarrassed, but then I dived into his arms and hugged him hard as I could, and felt him hug me back.

"Can you believe it?" said Luke. He couldn't stop chuckling to himself. "We really found it. In all this mess."

Hank studied the ticket some more, then finally slipped it into one of his front pockets. "I ain't ever gonna let this out of my sight again," he said. "No, sir."

I don't know how long we stayed in that Dumpster

celebrating and carrying on, but eventually someone decided that rich people like us ought to find a better place to throw a party, and so we climbed on out, tired, beat, and worn out, but nevertheless happy as hogs in slop.

Laughing, joking, and slapping each other on the back, we came around the side of the Dumpster and suddenly found ourselves staring into the crazed face of a skinny scarecrow of a man with wild, bloodshot eyes.

GREEDY GRADY

He stood there, arms outstretched, barring our way.

"Didja get the ticket?" he cackled. His eyes danced about in their sockets like red diamonds. "Didja, miss?"

For a moment I found myself frozen between confusion and horror. Then I recognized him as Grady, the bum I'd seen earlier at the market, and my expression changed from surprise to disgust.

"What did you do? Follow me here?" I asked.

"Just wanted to make sure no harm came to you," he said. He leaned in close and whispered hoarsely. "I got some information on the Pittsburgh Steelers that could be worth a fortune. Still not too late to go partners.''

''I told you we're done gambling,'' I said.

Hank put one arm around Luke and another around me. ''If you'll please excuse us,'' he said, ''we have business to attend to.''

Grady bowed and gestured with his hand for us to pass. ''Wouldn't want to stand in the way of business, but if you change your mind . . . well, don't forget I can make you rich.''

We walked away without replying, and when I looked back a minute or two later, he'd disappeared.

''Jamie, you meet some of the weirdest people,'' said Luke. ''Who was that, anyway?''

''His name's Grady,'' I said. ''Remember that burned-out gambler I told you was in the market this morning? Well, that's him. He is a little weird, isn't he?''

''I guess,'' said Luke, rolling his eyes.

''I'll feel better once that ticket is cashed,'' said Hank. ''All the freaks around here give me the creeps.'' He smiled, showing off his Dracula teeth. ''Know what I mean?''

We all laughed. ''Say, Hank, want to ride with us as far as St. George?'' I said. ''It's on the way to Colorado.''

''Colorado?'' said Hank.

''Your granddaughter,'' I said. ''Don't you want to take her the money?''

"Ummm ... yeah, but ..." stammered Hank.

"For her operation, remember," I said.

Hank shook his head, then sighed. "Jamie, I'm afraid I don't have a granddaughter. Never did."

"You what ... ?" said Luke.

We'd come to a stop in the middle of the parking lot.

"Hank, but then—"

"No granddaughter," he said sadly. He fiddled around in one of his pockets and drew out some nuts. "The whole thing was made up. I'm sorry if I lied. Believe me."

He looked away and fumbled nervously with the pistachios. Luke and I exchanged glances, with Luke's saying *See, I told you so.*

I was stunned cold. "But then what was the money for?"

"For a nest egg," said Hank. "At my age I knew no one would ever give me a job. Whatever savings I could put together was going to have to last. Twenty thousand, I figured, was the minimum I was going to need."

"But you didn't have to lie," I said. "We didn't care."

"Maybe, but I did," said Hank. "Putting my life savings down on the red seemed just plain stupid, probably was plain stupid. But I'd convinced myself I had to do it. So why should I have admitted it to a couple of perfect strangers? It didn't seem necessary."

"It never did make sense to me," said Luke.

"Well, I believed it," I said.

"I just never thought we'd stick together so long. Never thought the lie would matter." Hank lowered his head, then raised it back up. "Does it?"

I sighed. "Forget about it. I guess we've all done some stupid things these last few days. Me as much as anyone."

We exchanged smiles and started once again for the casino. "So, tell me, Mr. Moneybags, what are you planning to do next?"

"Go into business," he said.

"Business?" I said. "Not with that Grady fellow, I hope?"

He laughed. "Nope, with your grandpa, if he's interested."

I was stunned. "Grandpa?"

"Ever since you first mentioned him, he's been on my mind," said Hank. "I've been itching to get back to prospecting for years now, and that uranium field outside of Durango is ripe for the picking. Do you think he'd want to go partners?"

"I'd be surprised if he didn't," said Luke. "It's just what he needs to cheer him up."

Hank winked. "Me too."

"I got to warn you, though," said Luke. "Grandpa can be kind of ornery."

"Me too," said Hank. "Us prospectors are all a little bullheaded. Comes with the job." We'd paused just outside the door to the casino. "No, don't worry about us. I think we're going to get along just fine."

"Me too," I said.

The glass doors to the casino parted before us and we strode into the Firebird. That place never ceased to amaze me. Once inside you never saw a window or a clock, so no matter the time, day or night, it was always the same. The same smoke, same noises, same shouts, same smell. It could have been thirty degrees below zero outside or a hundred and thirty above and you'd never know it. The town could be ablaze, a foreign army marching through the streets, or frogs raining from the sky, but inside the Firebird it would always be Gambling World and Gambling Time. Like another world, which it was.

At the bottom of Hank's ticket it said the Firebird owed him just over twenty-two thousand dollars, but we walked away from the cashier with something considerably less. As the clerk explained, payoffs that size come to the attention of the Internal Revenue Service. They made Hank fill out a pile of forms and then took about a third of his money off the top for taxes. The way I saw it, it was just another lesson in the foolishness of gambling. Think about it. Even when we won we lost! It didn't seem right, but there was nothing we could do about it.

When we got back to Hank's room, Luke called Mom to tell her we would soon be leaving. As he chattered away, filling her in on all that had happened, and letting her know that Hank was coming to lift Grandpa out of the doldrums, I wandered over to the little table near the partially opened window and watched Hank count out hundred-dollar bills into two neat piles.

He was still going at it when Luke came over and handed me the phone. "Mom wants to talk to you," he said.

"Hi, Mom," I said. "How are you doing?"

"I can't tell you how relieved I am that everything is at last all right," she said. "You don't know how worried I've been."

"I have a pretty good idea," I said.

"From what Luke says, your friend is going to be just what Grandpa needs," she said. "I'm so pleased."

"We'll see you soon," I said. "Your worrying days are over."

Just then there was a knock at the door and Luke got up to answer it.

"Jamie, before I hang up I want to know if you've heard the joke about the rope?"

As I was deciding whether I wanted to really hear her silly joke, Luke opened the door and a skinny wild-eyed man holding a shotgun burst into the room and screamed, "Fork over that money! It's a stickup!"

I guess Mom could hear the shouting over the phone, because I heard her let out a scream—a series of screams, actually.

"Jamie! What is it?" she sputtered.

"It's—it's Grady," I replied. "He's got a—a gun!"

"Grady! Grady who?" she screeched.

Out of the corner of my eye I saw Hank sweep the money from the table onto the windowsill, where, for the moment, it remained hidden from Grady's view.

"Answer me! Jamie! Are you all right?"

"So far," I whispered. "But the guy's got a shotgun and I think he—"

Whap! With his free hand Grady seized the phone and ripped the cord from the wall.

Mom, of course, was cut off, but I almost thought I could hear her shrieks anyway, all the way from St. George. I guess her worries weren't meant to be over. Or ours.

"I said fork it over!" roared Grady. He hurled the phone to the floor and I nearly leapt onto the table.

"Now, just take it easy," said Luke, raising his arms.

"Give me the money!" screamed Grady. "Give it up or I'm going to start shooting."

12

THE
ROPE JOKE

I hadn't seen many shotguns in my life, but I'd seen
enough to know that Grady's looked pretty authentic.
Even if it had looked like a toy, I'm not sure I would
have tried to call his bluff. As my father once said,
"Don't do anything crazy when someone's got a gun,
especially when you think that someone might be crazy
himself."

"All right!" said Grady. There was sweat on his
brow and madness and fear in his big round eyes. "I
know you turned in that ticket. Hand over the cash."

Hank stood up and began fumbling in his pockets.

"All right, all right," he said. "Calm down, young fellow. No need getting all twitchy, now."

"Just fork it over, old man."

Hank went slowly from pocket to pocket, pretending to look for the money. "Got to be here somewhere," he kept saying, pulling out yet another handful of pistachios. "Just don't shoot. I know I'm going to find it."

He was stalling for time, but I couldn't figure out what time was going to buy us. The phone had been yanked out of the wall, the door was closed, and the only person who knew we were in trouble was Mom and she didn't know where we were, because Hank had paid for the room and registered us under his own name. I guess I could have stuck my head out the window and yelled down to the people walking along the Fabulous Las Vegas Strip to come save us, but I don't think Grady would have permitted me more than a word or two before pulling the trigger and shutting my trap.

I looked down at the bills sitting by the window and considered handing them over. Money wasn't worth getting killed over, that was the kind of thing my father might say, but ...

My father!

Why, he would know what to do. A man like my dad was never at a loss when it came to attracting attention. Hadn't he attracted a ton of attention at the Hotel del Coronado? And done the same a week earlier at the Ritz? That was where, you might remember, he'd whirled about the restaurant filling the air with dollar bills. The Ritz Trick, we'd called it, and it was just what I had in mind to alert the police to our current predicament.

While Grady nervously watched Hank going through his hundreds of pockets, finding a few dollars here, an old pack of gum there, and pistachios everywhere, I began pushing hundred-dollar bills out the window. Leaning against the sill I watched them lazily float six stories to the street, where, even before they began to hit, they managed to attract a crowd of half a dozen excited people. Frenzied, people, really, running, shouting, pointing, and leaping into the air. My dad had taught me that people would do most anything for money, and was he ever right. The citizens of the fair city of greed were going nuts. Absolutely nuts.

Within minutes people were running toward the Firebird from every direction imaginable. A nearby restaurant emptied out as if its insides were ablaze. Drivers abandoned their cars in the middle of the street, and I even saw two clowns and an acrobat come dashing over from the nearby Circus Circus Hotel.

"I'm running out of patience," snarled Grady. He pointed the gun my way and aimed. "Cough up that cash. Now."

I glanced at the gun, then down at the street, and my heart leapt. Two policemen had just emerged from their squad car. One of them was pointing up at our room. A moment later they both disappeared, at a run, into the hotel.

"You got to the count of ten," said Grady. "One . . . two . . . three . . . four . . ."

Hank and I exchanged worried looks. "Five . . . six . . . seven . . . I'm dead serious," he said. "And if you don't come through, this little lady here is going to be just plain dead—seriously dead . . . eight . . ."

I shut my eyes and then opened them a second later when Hank said, "The money's on the sill. Take it and get out. Just don't shoot."

Grady showed us a mouthful of yellow teeth and crossed to the window. He scooped up what was left of the bills and shoved them into his pocket.

"Now, go on," said Hank. He waved at the door. "Get out."

Grady licked at his lips and now a dangerous gleam came into his eye. "Can't have any witnesses," he said.

He pointed the gun again at me, but before he could shoot, Luke brought him up short. "Don't be stupid, Grady. You're never going to get away with this."

"Huh?" said Grady, spinning about, leveling the gun at Luke, standing alongside the bed. "What are you talking about, kid?" I held my breath. I had the uncomfortable feeling that Grady intended to pull the trigger if Luke's answer didn't satisfy him. "Don't be a fool. The sound of that gun going off will bring every security man in this hotel running, the cops too," said Luke.

Grady narrowed his eyes.

"Even if you got out of here, you couldn't get far.

The police will chase you into the desert. It's a hundred and fifty out there—in the shade.''

Grady licked at his lips, caught up now in the horrible picture Luke had begun to paint.

"There will be no water. Not a drop. Your tongue will start to swell up—"

"Shut up, kid!" said Grady. His eyes darted about nervously. I think Luke had him genuinely worried.

"I'm telling you," said Luke. "You take that money and you're going to end up fried out in the desert, lizards will be nibbling on your toes and—"

Bang! Bang! Bang! "Open up in there! It's the police!"

I smiled. "What did I tell you," said Luke.

Grady glared at Luke and his finger twitched against the trigger. "You—you—" he stammered. The police pounded on the door again and Grady looked about the room in desperation, searching for a way out. At last his eyes fell on the closet.

"The police! We want to talk to you in there!"

"Don't nobody say a word," whispered Grady. He waved the gun in our faces for a final time and backed himself into the closet, leaving the door open just enough so that the gun barrel was sticking out, and pointed at me. "All right," he growled. "Get rid of those cops."

"You're the boss," said Hank. He crossed the room and opened the door. "Yes, officers?" he said.

"Someone in this room has been tossing hundred-dollar bills out the window," said a red-faced policeman.

"Hundred-dollar bills!" said Hank with genuine surprise.

Grady kept his gun pointed right at me. But he couldn't see Luke, who had slid silently across the bed and was now crawling along the carpet toward the closet.

"Mind if we look around?" asked the second policeman. "My name is Lieutenant García and my partner here is Sergeant Abel. If you don't mind, we'll only take a second."

"Well ... I ..." stammered Hank.

"Something wrong?" asked Sergeant Abel.

Now, in one swift move, Luke rolled to his back and kicked the closet door with such force that it caught Grady's shotgun midbarrel and jolted it out of his hands.

"Quick! The closet!" I yelled, and the policemen, guns drawn, came tumbling into the room.

Throwing open the closet door they dragged out Grady and quickly had him handcuffed. Hank, Luke, and I wound up on the opposite side of the room, in each other's arms.

"Mind telling us what's been going on?" said Lieutenant García.

After I'd explained everything, Hank asked the police officers how they knew we were being robbed.

Officer García walked to the window and looked out. "Come here," he said. "You'll see."

Hank and Luke were stunned. And even I was a little surprised by the scene taking place below our window. There must have been at least two or three hundred people milling about the sidewalk with dozens more hurrying to join them. Traffic on the strip had come to a complete standstill. The clowns and the acrobat I'd seen earlier had now been joined by other performers from the Circus Circus, including a lady in a silver dress and five similarly dressed dogs, undoubtedly all part of the same act.

As soon as they saw us looking down they began to chant, in unison, "More money! More money! More money!" I had to laugh to myself. They were yelling the Las Vegas fight song, the gamblers' cry. "More money! More money! More money!"

"Sorry, Hank," I said. "I threw a bunch of your money out of the window. It was the only way I knew to save our necks." I looked at Luke. "The Ritz Trick," I added.

By the time Hank got his money back from Grady and counted it up he discovered he had just under twelve thousand dollars, about what he'd come to town with.

"Think we'll get any of those hundred-dollar bills back?" I asked.

"More money! More money! More money!" cried the crowd.

"What do you think?" said Officer García, smiling.

While we were busy answering questions from the police, some people from the hotel came by, including my old acquaintance, Mr. Henniman.

"Looks like you made a pile of money after all," he said, staring down at me with those creepy coal-black eyes of his. "Enough, it seems, to throw a wad of it away. What happened? Make another bet?"

"Same bet," I said. "I just didn't realize we'd won all along."

Mr. Henniman raised an eyebrow. "Same ILLE-GAL bet?" he said.

I gulped. "Well, I didn't really ..."

Mr. Henniman held out his 'hand. "Hand it over. You said yourself it never should have counted."

"But—but—" I looked desperately to Hank, then to Luke.

Mr. Henniman smiled and gave me one of his grand-fatherly pats. "Just kidding," he said. "You probably threw most of your winnings out the window anyway. The Firebird couldn't have asked for better advertising. Miss Plufphanger, you're welcome to stay here any-time you want—on the house."

"Thanks," I said, "but I don't think I'll be back for a while. Las Vegas isn't exactly my kind of town. Be-sides, my poor mother ..." My hand flew to my cheek. "Oh, no! My mother!" I exclaimed. "She must be wor-ried sick."

And, of course, she was. I called her almost imme-diately from a phone next door. It must have taken at least ten minutes for Luke and me to calm her down. In the end Officer García came on the phone to finally assure her that both her children were, indeed, still in one piece.

"Yes, Mrs. Plufphanger, they're both fine," said the officer. "Actually, rather than be upset you should be proud—they're heroes, these two.... Yes, yes, I'll see to it myself that they get on their way.... Leaving in an hour. I'll see to it.... The rope? Yes, I'll tell them. Good-bye."

Eventually the room emptied out till only the three of us and Officer García remained.

"I promised your mother I'd see you to your car," he said. "Are you and your grandfather ready to go?"

"I'm ready," said Luke.

"Me too," said Hank, "but you got us wrong, Lieutenant García. I'm not the children's grandfather."

"Oh?" said Lieutenant García.

I put my arm around Hank's waist. "Well, maybe he's not our real grandfather, but he's family just the same." I looked up at Hank and beamed. "How does honorary grandpa sound?"

"Honorary grandpa?"

"Sure, why not?"

Hank's eyes filled with tears. "I—I never had a family before." He put his hand on my shoulder. "I'd be proud to be your grandfather, Jamie." He looked at my brother. "Yours, too, Luke."

"Grandpa Hank. I like the ring of that," said Luke.

"Then it's official," I said. "From now on you're going to be a Plufphanger. How's that feel?"

"The name's going to take some getting used to. But the feeling? Well, that's first rate, Jamie. Yes, sir, first rate."

Lieutenant García picked up our suitcase and cleared his throat, loudly. "I'm sorry, but we really do have to be going."

"The sooner the better, as far as I'm concerned," said Luke. "I want to get there before dark. Driving up through those hills around St. George can be dangerous even during the day. Not only do you have to look out for rockslides, there's deer all over the place and even coyotes sometimes. And in a rainstorm—"

I laughed. "Luke! Listen to yourself. There you go worrying again. When's the last time your worrying ever did us any good?"

"Just an hour ago it happened to have saved your life," said Luke. "If I hadn't gone on about the desert and the lizards and the police, Grady would have shot us all. No doubt about it."

"Luke's right," said Hank. "We owe him our thanks."

I nodded. "You were kind of special back there. I'll admit it."

"Wasn't that Grady something, though?" said Hank. "A ruined gambler, I guess. At the end of his rope."

"Heavens, that reminds me," said Officer García. "Your mother told me to be sure and tell you the rope joke."

"What about the rope?" asked Luke.

"Skip it," said Lieutenant García.

118

"No, no, tell us," I said. "What's the rope joke?"

"Skip it. Skip it!" said the officer.

I groaned. "That does it. Absolutely positively I'm getting Mom a decent joke book as soon as we get to St. George."

"And I'll be more than happy to chip in," said Luke.

"Me too," said Officer García.

We headed for the car. I probably didn't have five dollars to my name, but I felt like the richest kid in town. My family had just grown, and my grandpa was going to be okay. Hank too. In spite of everything, I had to be the biggest winner in the history of Las Vegas.

ABOUT THE AUTHOR

Stephen Mooser is the founder and president of the Society of Children's Books Writers. He is the author of many books, including *101 Black Cats* and, for Dell Yearling, *Shadows on the Graveyard Trail*. He lives in Bar Harbor, Maine.